PRAISE FOR *̶ ̶ ̶ ̶*̶

'A literary phenomenon.' *Guardian*

'By aı

Telegrapn

'A superb demonstration of Rendell's talent for spotting the contradictions in human nature.' *Daily Mail*

'Every [story] is a gem ... *A Spot of Folly* shines as a superb epitaph to Rendell's talent, reflecting the breadth and richness of her unique ability to turn seemingly ordinary everyday situations into suspenseful masterpieces ... the perfect book to curl up with in front of a log fire with a glass of wine.' *Daily Express*

'Wickedly macabre ... these strong, atmospheric stories convey a sardonic message.' *Observer*

'Rendell, that most missed of crime writers, seems to have a rare and uncanny ability to understand what people are really like; and every so often there comes an unnerving moment when you feel her all-seeing gaze has expanded to encompass not just her characters but you yourself.' *Daily Telegraph*

'She was a remarkable writer, who recorded the pain of the unhappy, the ungenerous and unloved.' Natasha Cooper, *TLS*

'Deliciously riveting ... Miraculously "hookish"' Sarah Perry, author of *The Essex Serpent*

RUTH RENDELL was one of the great crime writers. Her books – notable for their careful psychological observation, as well as their gripping plots – have sold over 20 million copies worldwide, and she won numerous awards, including the Crime Writers' Association Cartier Diamond Dagger for sustained excellence in crime writing. In 1996 she was awarded the CBE and in 1997 became a Life Peer. Ruth Rendell died in May 2015.

A Spot of Folly

Ten Tales of Murder and Mayhem

RUTH RENDELL

PROFILE BOOKS

This paperback edition published in 2018

First published in Great Britain in 2017 by
PROFILE BOOKS LTD
3 Holford Yard
Bevin Way
London
WC1X 9HD
www.profilebooks.com

'Never Sleep in a Bed Facing a Mirror', first published in the *Daily Telegraph*, 8 February 1997;
'A Spot of Folly', first published in *Ellery Queen's Mystery Magazine*, November 1974; 'The Price
of Joy', first published in *Ellery Queen's Mystery Magazine*, April 1977; 'The Irony of Hate', first
published in *Winter's Crimes 9*, 1977 and then in *The Best of Winter's Crimes, Volume 2*, 1986;
'Digby's Wives', first published in *Woman's Own*, January 1985; 'The Haunting of Shawley
Rectory', first published in *Ellery Queen's Mystery Magazine*, December 1979; 'A Drop Too
Much', first published in *Winter's Crimes 7*, 1975; 'The Thief', first published by Arrow in 2006;
'The Long Corridor of Time', first published in *Ellery Queen's Mystery Magazine*, February
1974; 'In the Time of his Prosperity' (as Barbara Vine), first published in *Ellery Queen's Mystery
Magazine*, August 2005; 'Trebuchet', first published in *The Listener Magazine*, July 1985

Selection copyright © Tony Medawar, 2017, 2018
Introduction copyright © Sophie Hannah, 2017, 2018

1 3 5 7 9 10 8 6 4 2

Printed and bound in Great Britain by CPI Group (UK) Ltd, Croydon CR0 4YY

A CIP record for this book can
be obtained from the British Library

ISBN 978 1 78816 015 5
eISBN 978 1 78283 429 8

Mixed Sources
Product group from well-managed
forests and other controlled sources
www.fsc.org Cert no. TT-COC-002227
© 1996 Forest Stewardship Council
FSC

Contents

Introduction

Strictly speaking, when I was asked to write the introduction for this collection of Ruth Rendell short stories, I should have said no. As a devoted Rendell fan, I was hugely tempted, but busy with other projects and stressed about deadlines. I nearly did say no – until I remembered that reading Ruth Rendell was what I did for many years while I was supposed to be doing other more soul-destroying and oppressive things. Reading Ruth Rendell was what saved me from alienation and disillusion during my student days. Besides, if I said no, I would have to wait until the publication date to read these exciting stories that I hadn't known existed, whereas if I said yes, I would get to read them immediately. To cut a long story short … it turned out that I couldn't resist.

I first discovered Rendell when I was supposed to be doing no such thing – I was supposed to be working. During my gap year I worked for Manchester Theatres Limited, where my job was to distribute leaflets around the city centre, advertising our shows.

Illicit shopping was far more fun, however, so one day, instead of leafletting, I ventured into Hatchards bookshop. There I found two whole rows of Ruth Rendell novels. I knew from my first glance at the blurbs that this was a writer I would be spending a lot of time with. I bought *From Doon with Death*, the first Inspector Wexford novel, and loved it. But then I must have been distracted by other things, because I didn't immediately read any more. Silly me.

A year later, I went to university, and very much didn't want to be there – I was on the wrong course, one I had chosen based on what I'd been told I was good at, not what I wanted to do, and I felt thoroughly miserable. I'm not exaggerating when I say that buying the set texts for that course made me feel physically sick. Good old Ruth Rendell came to my rescue. The set texts bookshop had a fiction section, containing a row of Rendells. In that moment, I knew that these books, and not *Don Quixote*, were what I would be immersing myself in for the next few years.

The hookiness of Rendell's writing was something I hadn't experienced since discovering Agatha Christie at the age of twelve. I started to collect the books, including those written as Barbara Vine, and bought a new bookcase specially for that purpose. Very soon, Rendell was up there with Enid Blyton and Agatha Christie on my official Favourite Authors Of All Time list. I watched *Inspector Wexford* on television, bought a cassette tape of the soundtrack and listened to it non-stop in the car. It drove my boyfriend mad. I went to see Rendell speaking at Waterstones in Manchester, and she said something I've never forgotten: that it's vital to hook the reader from the very first line. If the first line is not gripping, the reader won't persevere.

And boy, was Rendell gripping. The first line of *A Judgement in Stone*, the first paragraph of *A Dark-Adapted Eye* (a Barbara Vine book), the amazing twist in *The Secret House of Death*, the atmospheric blending of past and present in *Asta's Book* ... the list could go on and on. In Rendell's universe, oddness is absolutely commonplace. It's everywhere, and fascinating; it's in all of us, however hard we try to hide it. There is no (good) Us and (evil) Them — we're all desperately trying to seem normal and functional while wrestling with twisted obsessions and weird preoccupations. For this reason, many readers don't find Rendell's fiction reassuring enough, but I've always felt the opposite. Rendell gets it. She doesn't tidy people up in fiction. She understands that most real people are far weirder than most novels allow their protagonists to be. As a reader, I can only feel reassured around those writers who truly understand how dysfunctional humans are.

Rendell mastered the short story form as well as the novel, publishing seven original short story collections in her lifetime. The stories in this collection are previously uncollected, and each one is a miracle of narrative construction — shapely, taut, suspenseful. She offers the same narrative satisfaction in her stories as she does in her novels, which is not true of all writers. Many short stories give us simply a slice of life, a snapshot of a moment. Rendell's, in contrast, have beginnings, middles and ends and they keep you on the edge of your seat throughout.

The stories in this book are amazingly gripping. Many protagonists, despite being devious themselves, are oddly naive. They run into trouble because they imagine everyone around them is more virtuous and less calculating than they themselves are. They fail, in one story after another, to make the imaginative leap from knowing what they're capable of to working out that others might be capable of similar immorality.

A recurring theme is the human ego and the harm it can do. In the title story, 'A Spot of Folly', the protagonist cheats on his wife and has dalliances with other women mainly so that he can boast to his male colleagues – if he doesn't get to boast, he seems to feel that his sexual prowess almost doesn't count. Most of the stories feature people who imagine they're more in control of their lives than they in fact are. They break interpersonal and social contracts thinking that they're unique, that everyone else will play along – but time and time again, Rendell's protagonists discover that promise-breakers attract other promise-breakers. The law of karma is strong in these stories – nobody gets away with anything. The protagonist in 'The Price of Joy' undervalues what he has simply because he has it; he values what he's discarded and can't get back. This book is full of unrestrained ego and all its satisfying narrative possibilities.

Traditional crime fiction, say some, offers the satisfaction of good triumphing over evil, while a lot of contemporary crime invites readers to sympathise equally with the victim and the perpetrator. Rendell chooses a third option in these stories, and shows that often killer and victim are equally dreadful and that it's foolish to care about either. It's easy to say that Rendell is a misanthrope, but that's a simplistic reading of her work. Rather, she appears to be saying that there is a self-seeking and remorseless streak in human nature of which we must all beware. She brings to life the worst that could happen, always springing from dangerous delusions and disastrous decisions. To claim that she painted all people as awful is as daft as suggesting that Edgar Degas believed all women should be ballet dancers.

There are three ghost stories in this collection. 'Never Sleep in a Bed Facing a Mirror' is three lines long and is superb. Utterly chilling, it shows us how much can be communicated in very few words. It's the best tiny story I've ever read, even better than Ernest Hemingway's famous six-worder about baby shoes. The other two ghost stories here are longer: one is conventional, one isn't. In both, ghosts take on the role played by the human ego in the non-supernatural stories, and cause people to commit dreadful crimes.

The last story here – about a family in denial of what they know to be true: that the world is about to end after some kind of nuclear disaster – is the perfect chilling note to end on. The protagonists don't mention their impending doom, and pretend they don't know what's happened. In this final story, we start to feel that any delusions we harbour, whether ghostly or egotistical, might be entirely understandable in the face of the horror all around us – which might be nuclear destruction, as in this story, or it might be what we know of the world, life, death and other people.

It's rare, from my perhaps-not-sufficiently-highbrow perspective, to find a collection of short stories that's as satisfying as a novel, but this one passes the test with flying colours. It's the perfect addition to all Rendell fans' collections and the perfect starting point for those who are new to her work.

Sophie Hannah

Never Sleep in a Bed
Facing a Mirror

Alone in the four-poster, she glanced up from her book and saw in the mirror a little old woman sitting beside her. She shut her eyes, looked again, saw an empty bed, neatly made with fresh linen. The hotel staff, summoned by her screams, found no one, not even herself.

A Spot of Folly

The other delegates to the sales conference were spending the evening at the Folies Bergère and going on afterward to some night club. Unless he could scrape up an acquaintance in the bar, which the language barrier made unlikely, there would be no one to whom he could relate his experience of the past few hours. As he drove the Renault into the underground car park, Sandy Vaughan considered this with a shade of bitterness that threatened to eclipse his triumphant mood. To tell his sort of story when it is fresh in the mind – and the body – is everything. Much is lost by waiting till next day. A gloom descends on it in inverse ratio to the brightness of the morning light, and that which has evinced one's worldly wisdom and conquering charm at midnight becomes stale, flat and unprofitable at 7:30 in the morning.

The foyer of the Hotel Toronto, to which Sandy ascended by elevator, was dimly lit. The night porter sat behind the reception desk reading *France Soir* and smoking a small black cigar. Sandy asked for his room key and was going back to the elevator when he noticed there was still a light on in the bar. A little nightcap – a double whiskey, say – would send him to sleep and console him for the lack of companionship. The bar seemed to be empty except for the barman, a sullen-looking youth, occupied precisely as was the night porter.

Sandy pushed open the double glass doors. He got halfway to the bar and then saw that the place wasn't, as he'd first believed, deserted. At a table in a far corner, an empty glass and a full ashtray in front of him, sat Denis Crawford looking, Sandy thought, as if he'd lost a thousand francs on a dud lottery ticket. But this did nothing to deter Sandy. He was delighted to find so unexpectedly a friend and a listener. He charged across the room, waving jovially as if he hadn't seen Denis for a year.

'Well, well, well,' he chuckled, slapping Denis on the back. 'Fancy finding you here!'

'I'm staying here,' said Denis.

'I know you are, old man, but I thought you'd gone off with the boys to the Folies.'

'I don't much care for that sort of thing.' Shoved, dug in the ribs, Denis edged away along the upholstered seat.

'Didn't you go?'

Sandy had been hoping for just such an opening. Slightly lowering his voice, leaning closer, he said, 'I've been having a little spot of follies on my own account.'

Denis said nothing. His look indicated that he thought Sandy had been to a strip show, a misapprehension Sandy intended to dispel. 'Wait till you hear, old man,' he said. 'But a drink first, eh?'

'I don't want another, thanks, Sandy.'

'Nonsense, of course you do.' He shouted, '*Garçon!*' to the barman whose face became even more sullen at this term of address. '*Deux* whiskey sours,' and he held up two fingers in case there should be any doubt.

Denis said, 'I don't think he much cares for being called that.'

'Then he must lump it, old man. My French may not be up to your standards – I didn't have the advantage of going to school in France – but I flatter myself it's adequate, perfectly adequate.'

'I'm sure you manage, Sandy.'

Here was another excellent cue. 'I do that all right, Den, old boy. My not *parlez*-ing like a bloody French dictionary didn't stand in my way tonight, I can tell you. There is one activity you can get by in with a universal language, and you won't need three guesses to tell me what that is.'

The barman slapped down the whiskey sours and while Sandy muttered a curt '*Merci,*' Denis let forth a flood of which Sandy caught the gist, that he was apologizing for keeping that sulky boy up so late. The barman's face registered a slightly warmer expression. Sandy shrugged impatiently at the diversion. He took a swig at his drink and tried again.

'By God, I need that after what I've been up to.'

'Well, what have you been up to?'

Sandy didn't much care for the way Denis had said that, with a half sigh as if he were bored. Denis Crawford had better remember he was a junior executive of the firm, that he'd been with them only nine months, and that it was only because of his French and Sandy's kind string-pulling that he was here in Paris at all. 'I'll tell you, my lad. I've been up to what I get up to whenever I find myself at a loose end in a big city – to wit, passing a highly enjoy-able evening in the arms of a very sweet chick.'

'You what?' said Denis.

'Come on now, laddie, you heard. I was all set to go along to the Folies with the boys, but I had ten minutes to kill so I popped into this bar in Montmartre for a quick one. The next thing I knew there was this chick giving me the eye. And was she an eyeful herself!' Sandy chuckled reminiscently.

'We went back to her place, a lovely little flat right up at the top of Montmartre, and then – well, you can imagine. I don't need to go into details.'

But he went into a few just the same. 'I'd have stayed all night, as a matter of fact, but she was expecting her boyfriend home at half-past eleven. I didn't fancy any rough stuff, and he's of a jeal-ousy *formidable*, she said. But it was a real wrench tearing myself away from a chick like that.'

To Sandy's amusement Denis had flushed darkly. He seemed quite upset, almost as if he'd had a shock, and when he reached for a cigarette his hand was unsteady. At last he said in a very low voice, 'Do you make a habit of this sort of thing?'

'When I'm out of England, I told you. What's so terrible about that? A man needs a bit of comfort after a hard day's work.'

'I never knew. I hadn't the faintest idea.' Really, you'd have thought Sandy had confessed to some crime, some nasty perver-sion. Sandy started to laugh at the man's naivety, but Denis' next question made him almost cross. 'What does Diana say about these – these goings-on?'

'You don't suppose I let my wife into secrets of that sort?'

'But she loves you, she's devoted to you.'

'So she should be,' said Sandy, peeved by this censorious inqui-
sition. 'I've given her two smashing little kids, haven't I? And a
damn sight better house than her father ever had, and a car of her
own and whatever she likes to spend on clothes. What more does
she expect?'

Denis Crawford hadn't yet touched his drink. He raised his
right arm now in a funny gesture as if to ward off a blow and in
letting it fall across the table as he uttered the single word, 'Fidel-
ity,' he swept his glass and its contents to the floor. There was a
tinkling crash and a little pool of liquid on the carpet. It was, of
course, pure accident, as Sandy, not sorry for this interruption,
hastened to say.

The barman put down his paper, got off his stool, and came
over to pick up the broken glass. He regarded the carpet in gloomy
doubt, thought better of any notion of swabbing up the liquid, and
instead smudged it further in with his toe.

'*Encore, un* whiskey sour,' said Sandy.

'Not for me. I'm going to bed.'

Sandy watched him go. He didn't cancel the order but drank it
himself. Well, he'd know better than to confide in Denis Crawford
again, the miserable milksop. Sandy liked this alliterative combi-
nation so much that he repeated it several times under his breath
– miserable milksop, miserable mealy-mouthed milksop.

Of course all that sort of moralistic disapproval could be put
down to envy. Denis might be tall and dark and good-looking
and only twenty-eight, but he hadn't the faintest idea how to go
about life. And Sandy remembered how dim he'd been when he'd
first come to London and had stayed with him and Diana before
he'd found a place of his own. Even then he'd refused all Sandy's

friendly overtures and offers to show him the town, preferring to go to those way-out cinemas or stay in with Diana and the kids. Poor old Diana, she must have got pretty fed up with him following her about like a little dog.

Yes, Denis Crawford was a poor thing. Couldn't drink, never had a woman, didn't know he was born. Might even be queer. This thought cheered Sandy so much that he condescended to say a jolly *'Bon soir'* to the barman before going upstairs and falling into a heavy sleep.

On the following day they got up from the conference table at lunchtime, and Sandy, not at all anxious to join the others in an organized trip up the Eiffel Tower, made for the telephone. First he called his wife. He knew his duty. It was one thing to have a bit of fun when one was off the leash, quite another to neglect one's wife. Sandy had nothing but contempt for men who neglected their wives. Poor old Diana worried herself sick about him if he didn't call regularly.

'Hello, darling,' he said in hearty cheerful tones when she answered. 'How's tricks?'

Funny creatures, women, you never quite knew how they'd react. She'd moaned like hell when he'd told her the conference was going to last a whole week this year, yet now her 'Oh, it's you' sounded disappointed. For some reason. But it was no good letting them rile you and useless to probe into the causes of their funny little moods.

Instead he chatted breezily about Paris, giving her the impression he'd been out to Versailles and into some of those art galleries. When she'd told him the kids were all right and she was all right and he'd promised to bring her back some Rochas perfume, he hung up, his duty done. Now for pleasure.

Marie Laure's phone number was jotted down in the back of his address book, disguised under the clever code he always used. You took the two pairs of digits and subtracted ten from each pair. Simple, my dear Watson. I am Hawkshaw, the detective, and no one can pull a fast one on me. Sandy added the tens and dialed the decoded number.

She was in. *Evidemment*, she would love to see Song-dee that night. Would seven o'clock suit him? He understood, *n'est ce pas*, that the boyfriend would be home by ten, so he must be gone early, but if three hours of her company would suit him …?

Immensely pleased with himself, Sandy went up to the reception desk, asked to have his car washed, and cashed some traveller's cheques. In cataloguing Marie Laure's charms to Denis Crawford, he had omitted to mention that they were expensive. He went into the Avenue Kleber and bought a bottle of champagne. Then he had a bath and a little nap.

Sandy never went anywhere without having a quick one first. In the bar he encountered Denis Crawford drinking lager with Malcolm Shaw, the firm's marketing manager. Denis gave him such a cold truculent look that Sandy couldn't resist the temptation to tell them where he was going.

'That's my boy,' said Malcolm. 'You only live once.'

'If you call that living,' said Denis.

The other man winked at Sandy behind Denis' back. 'I'd have done the same myself, Sandy, a year ago. Still, I have my compensations.' He looked at his watch. 'Which reminds me it's time I gave her a call.'

Sandy watched him leave and hurry to the telephone.

'You see,' he said. 'I'm not the only one.'

'He's not married,' said Denis Crawford.

'Oh, you're too pure to live! No wonder the good people of Paris called a suburb after you. Saint Denis.' He laughed heartily at his joke. 'Personally, I prefer Montmartre and the Rue Ninon de l'Enclos.' And he got off his stool. 'See you.'

The Rue Ninon de l'Enclos was packed with cars, but Sandy managed to find a parking space. Marie Laure was waiting for him, his money, and his champagne, and gave him the sort of evening that always put him in high spirits. It was 9:55 when he came out into the street again and went back to his car.

A couple of yards from it he stopped short. There was a long jagged scrape on one of the Renault's fenders. He let out a gasp of anger and plunged forward, narrowly missing falling under the wheels of a taxi. The driver swore at him and Sandy swore back, shaking his fist. At close quarters the scrape was even worse than it had at first appeared. No doubt about it, that couldn't be merely sprayed. He'd have to have a new fender.

Sandy cursed richly. The French were wild drivers. Some madman, of that taxi-driver's type, had torn down the Rue Ninon de l'Enclos while Sandy was with Marie Laure and passed just too close to the Renault.

It wasn't until he was in the car, in the driver's seat, that he saw the note, a small scrap of paper held against the windshield by one of the wipers. Sandy put his hand out the window and took it, tearing it slightly as he pulled it from under the wiper. It read: *Thousand apologies. I will pay the damages. Meet me tomorrow 1900 hours Le Garage Rivery, Rue des Chattes, XVIIIme Arrondissement.*

There was no signature, no phone number. Still, it was enough.

It slightly consoled him for the scar on the Renault's virgin, jewel-like bodywork.

He found Malcolm Shaw sitting in the hotel lounge when he got back, and he showed him the note. 'Come and see what Monsieur Thousand Apologies has done,' he said, and together they went down to the car park. Denis Crawford would have to choose that moment to come into the car park and get something out of his own Mini. Sandy ignored him, even when he came up to them.

Malcolm made sympathetic noises. He agreed that the scrape was an eyesore, and together they prodded at the flaking paint. Denis wondered if the blow to the fender had upset the alignment, and although Sandy scoffed at this, he let Denis get into the car and shift about at the steering wheel, squinting absurdly through the windshield. Anything to keep him quiet. Malcolm made a few helpful suggestions and assessed the damage at about £50.

'You should get that out of him, Sandy,' he said. 'You always were lucky.'

'Better be born lucky than rich, eh?'

'You're lucky and rich.'

It was just like Denis Crawford to get out of the car at this point and interrupt their merriment with a grave, 'Has it occurred to you that this could be a trap?'

'A what?'

'A way of getting you on your own and beating you up. Maybe rob you as well.'

'And just why should Monsieur Thousand Apologies want to beat Sandy up?' asked Malcolm.

'Because the chances are he's the jealous lover of Sandy's lady friend.'

'Oh, you're crazy,' said Sandy. 'You go to the cinema too much.'

'Just think about it, Sandy. Why didn't he leave a name or a phone number on that note if he's honest? And why write in English? Yours is a French car.'

'He saw the G.B. plate, of course,' said Malcolm.

Denis shrugged. He scrutinized the fender. 'That wasn't made by another vehicle. It looks to me as if it was done with a hammer.'

'For God's sake!' Sandy exploded. 'How would you know? Since when have you been an insurance assessor? You've got an overdeveloped imagination, laddie.'

'All right. But I've warned you. You'd just better be careful.'

What a feeble character the man was! Neurotic, really. Sandy, who prided himself on his guts, felt rather stimulated than otherwise by Denis' forebodings. Not that he believed in them. But if there were something fishy about Monsieur Thousand Apologies, what an adventure, what a story to tell the boys! He pictured himself recounting the sort of experience that only a red-blooded man could have.

'Did I ever tell you about the time I had this French girl in Paris and her boyfriend came after me?' That was how he'd begin it. Savouring this story in anticipation, Sandy couldn't resist telling a good many of his colleagues about it on the following day. But in forecasting his own tactics he left out the gun.

The gun was a Luger that Sandy's father had taken off a dead German in 1940. His attitude toward it was much the same as other people's attitude toward sleeping pills. Though he had never used it, it was a comfort knowing it was there, and he never travelled without it. Ever since that time when he'd been threatened by a hitchhiker he'd picked up in Turkey, he'd taken the gun with him on his foreign trips, concealing it from the Customs by keeping it in a pocket under the passenger seat of the Renault. No one knew of its existence, not even Diana.

It often made Sandy chuckle when he thought of his car sitting in the garage at home, so innocent-looking, yet harbouring a lethal weapon. It was even more uproarious to recall that, out of the kindness of his heart, he'd lent the car to Denis a couple of times while he was staying with them. That miserable milksop would have turned even paler if he'd known about the gun.

But by the time he came to leave the hotel for his assignation, Sandy had decided that all danger lay in Denis' imagination. He'd telephoned the Garage Rivery during the day and found it to be authentic, and his first sight of it confirmed his own belief that it was respectable. It stood in one of the narrow dark streets that lie behind the Sacré Coeur; it wasn't small or dark but a modern well-lit establishment with the usual row of gas pumps and behind them a store and the sheds where repairs were made.

Sandy couldn't find a space to park the car on the garage fore-court without obstructing the way to the pumps, so he left it up against a wall that bordered the long alley between the store and the sheds.

There was no one in the garage office except the manager who succeeded in making Sandy understand that they were closing at 7:30. As it was only just 7:00 that left ample time to meet Monsieur Thousand Apologies and get the whole matter settled. Sandy chuckled to himself when he remembered Denis' forebodings. As if anything of that nature could happen in a well-lit much-frequented place like this.

He wondered rather scornfully where Denis was now. Sitting

by himself probably in a little dark cinema, watching the kind of French film Sandy would pay not to see, though he'd often paid well enough to see the other kind. Contentedly, he surveyed the cars which kept arriving for gas. One of them, sooner or later, would contain his man. He mustn't be impatient.

But when it got to be 7:20 and no one had turned up, when nobody had rushed in full of breathless apology and requests for an immediate examination of the Renault, he began to pace up and down the forecourt. They were preparing to close; a couple of mechanics were leaving and going off on motorbikes.

Sandy looked searchingly up and down the dark street. Although the street lamps were lit, the place had a sombre lonely look, overcast as it was by the rear of the great cathedral. There was no one about and no car but the Renault. When the manager turned off the lights and came out to lock up, there was nothing left for Sandy to do but to go and sit in his car.

Montmartre may be a place of gaiety near the Pigalle, of twinkling signs and lights as bright as fruit drops, of crowded bars and snug little theatres, but it is also a place of ancient darkness, a warren of deep lanes that seem chiselled into the hillside. Sandy couldn't help feeling vulnerable in his isolation, a target for easy violence in the one car left, and that car immediately identifiable by the mark that had been put on it.

After a few moments he switched off the interior light and reached under the seat for the Luger. Of course it was absurd, all his disquiet due to that fool Denis; but with the gun in his pocket he felt much more secure, and he settled down to wait once more.

It was 7:40 when he saw the man enter the garage forecourt. It was only a dim figure, heavily raincoated, but it was enough.

Monsieur Thousand Apologies at last, and he was alone. Well, they couldn't do much tonight – the place was closed thanks to the man's tardiness.

But that might stand him in good stead, Sandy thought. A man who was late and admittedly in the wrong would be in a false position to quibble. Sandy made up his mind that he'd settle for £50 and call it a day. He'd buy the bloke a drink in one of the bars he'd passed on his way up and then – why shouldn't he drop in on Marie Laure for a couple of hours?

He got out of the car, locking it carefully, and made his way past the gas pumps up to the office. The pallid lamplight was augmented by his own flashlight. He looked about him for the writer of the note, but he'd disappeared. Maybe they'd missed each other, and finding no one by the office, the man had made at once for the Renault he had so wantonly scarred.

Sandy went back. As before, the Rue des Chattes itself was deserted, empty of all vehicles. Monsieur Thousand Apologies hadn't come by car. Sandy thought he heard a footfall behind him and he wheeled. He turned rather sharply for one who felt as confident and in command of the situation as he did, and he gave a little laugh of reassurance at such an unexpected display of nerves.

His laugh was answered by a low dull snigger. Sandy froze. He put his hand to his pocket where the Luger was and started back toward the garage office.

The sound wasn't repeated.

Had it been only an echo, the reverberation of his own laugh thrown back by these walls? He took a deep breath and called out, 'Hello! Is anyone there? *Voila que j'y suis.* I'm here, by the office.'

A deep silence answered him. What the hell was the guy playing at? He was in here somewhere, he must be — Sandy had seen him come in. And now he began seriously to consider Denis' theory. Well, what if it were true? What if it was Marie Laure's lover who had crept up in the dark and was waiting to spring on him from behind one of those sheds? The man was alone, and Sandy had the Luger. That would be something to tell the boys, how he'd confronted this small-time gangster and sent him squealing off to his woman with his tail between his legs.

Resolutely, Sandy set off in search of Monsieur Thousand Apologies, treading softly and with great care down the long alley that ran between the main building and the repair sheds. It led finally into a small yard. He switched on his flashlight and surveyed this yard which was as gloomy and medieval-looking as the front was modern.

The thin beam of his flash shone on dilapidated black brickwork and sagging beams, flitted over a couple of empty doorways like the entrances to caves, lit up briefly a mountain of old car tires. From this heap of serpentine coils Sandy saw a shadow snake out and flicker into one of the caves.

He tensed and put the light out. Thrusting it into his left hand, he felt for the Luger with his right. A piece of timber creaked. Sandy slipped into the nearest cavern mouth and found himself in a brick tunnel. He closed his hand over the gun.

Immediately behind him — he came hard up against it — was a wooden door. Good, an excellent position to be in. Let Monsieur show himself now and he'd be ready for him. He brought the gun out and as his fingers tightened over it he felt on the metalwork an unaccustomed roughness as of sharp unfiled projections, like tiny thorns on its surface.

Although he had never actually fired the Luger, he had often handled it and taken pride in the perfection of its workmanship. Never had it felt like this. Cautiously, holding both under the hem of his jacket, he brought the light from the flash to bear on the gun. A shiver convulsed him and he almost cried out. It wasn't the Luger he was holding but a toy weapon, the kind children play with, exactly the kind, in fact, that his own boy played with. Could his son have discovered the Luger and substituted …? But there was no time to consider the awful possibilities of that now.

Sandy was trembling. He wouldn't be able to deceive a soul with this travesty of a weapon, and anyway he knew he'd never have the nerve to thrust it in a man's back while knowing it wasn't the genuine article. Besides, this man was a gangster, experienced in such things. Sandy would have to get out and get out fast.

A heavy sweat stood on his forehead. He put up his hand and wiped away the wetness. Why had he been such a fool as to come into this pitch-dark labyrinth without first checking the gun?

His legs unsteady, he came back to the mouth of the tunnel and into the black hole of a yard. He didn't dare put on the flashlight. He spreadeagled his body against the damp broken wall and eased himself along it, ducking behind the heap of slimy tires. There was no sound. At the point where he had seen the snaky shadow, he slipped into another tunnel, longer than the first which had given him sanctuary and which had seemed, while he was armed, so good a vantage place.

This tunnel was a passage at the end of which gleamed a faint light. Sandy began to run toward the light and had almost reached it when he heard a movement behind him. He flung himself hard against the wall and the bullet passed with terrifying swiftness, striking just where his head had been a second before and embedding itself in a wooden post.

He let out a cry of horror and sprang out of the passage into a pool of light. It came from a street lamp, but not one of those in the Rue des Chattes. Sandy didn't know where he was and he didn't care. There were no thoughts of subterfuge now, of trickery, but only of getting away, down, down into bright twinkling Montmartre whose sequinned glittering he could just see through a gap in towering walls.

He plunged through this gap, not daring to look behind him, and found himself on a terrace. Above him, white and gleaming, more like a mosque than a church, soared the towers of the Sacré Coeur. The great cathedral looked like a palace of ice. The floodlighting which was turned on it left a lake of darkness at Sandy's feet, and above this black waste hung the glittering lights of Paris, yellow and white and flickering fireworks-red.

He had never been into the Sacré Coeur, but he knew that a series of flights of steps fell away from this point to the street below, and below that, not too far away, was the Pigalle Metro station. Meanwhile he was an easy target for Marie Laure's gunman-lover.

Where was he now? Biding his time perhaps, or creeping up on him by some other way which he would know well. Sandy ran to the wall that surrounds the terrace and to the head of the flight of steps that leads down, through thick bushes, on the left-hand side. He had hardly reached the shelter of these winding narrow stairs and the obscurity of the bushes when he heard footfalls on the terrace. The footsteps moved slowly, hesitantly, as if the man who made them was uncertain, was searching.

Sandy clambered in among the shrubs, his hands scrambling

in earth, torn by the spines of a thorn tree. But now the footsteps were approaching with a sure firmness of purpose.

Could the man smell him? Was his ear so supernaturally sensitive that he'd heard the whisper of turned soil and the gush of blood from Sandy's prickled hand? Almost fainting now, Sandy cowered back. Wild thoughts of begging for mercy, of taking a beating so long as his life were spared, brought him to his knees, and he was on his knees, gasping, when the branches were pushed aside and he looked up into the eyes of Denis Crawford.

'You wished to see me, Monsieur le Commissaire?'

'You are very punctual, Monsieur Crawford. Please take a chair. First let me express the sympathies of the police department on the loss of your friend.'

Denis Crawford gave a slight grave nod. He sat down and faced the official across the polished desk.

'I doubt if I can help you, Monsieur,' Denis said. 'I went to the cinema last night and retired early to bed. I can only tell you what, I believe, my colleagues have already told you, that Monsieur Vaughan went out last night to keep an appointment with a man who had damaged his car.'

'But you were of the opinion, according to Monsieur Shaw, that this man was, in fact, the lover of a woman with whom Monsieur Vaughan had been having relations? Monsieur Shaw has told us you warned Monsieur Vaughan not to keep this decidedly suspicious appointment. How unfortunate your good advice was not taken! If it had been, Monsieur Vaughan would not have been found in the grounds of the Sacré Coeur this morning with a Luger bullet through his head. Another such bullet has been found in the woodwork of the Garage Rivery buildings. It would appear that Monsieur Vaughan was pursued but was not, alas, able to escape his attacker. You can throw no light on this man's identity, I suppose?'

'None, I regret. Monsieur Vaughan did not tell me this woman's name or address. But if the gun has been found, I foresee no difficulty in your tracing its owner.'

'Unfortunately, there will be great difficulty. How many Frenchmen possess such a weapon, obtained by themselves or their fathers *pendant la guerre?* During the war large numbers were taken from the bodies of German soldiers. No, *c'est difficile.* But we shall try, we shall make all efforts. The telephone number that we discovered in Monsieur Vaughan's address book – freshly inscribed there, we believe – is a Paris number but that of a most respectable dental surgeon. Nor do we know the numbers of the notes, five hundred francs, which Monsieur Shaw has informed me Monsieur Vaughan was carrying on him last night and of which he was robbed. So it will not, as you see, be an easy case. Now, Monsieur, you return to London today, do you not?'

'With your permission.'

'Certainly you have my permission. You are acquainted with the widow of Monsieur Vaughan?'

'I know her slightly.'

'Then will you do the police department the great service of returning to this unfortunate lady certain possessions of her husband, his watch, his wedding ring, and so on?'

'It will be, Monsieur le Commissaire, if not a pleasure, a willingly undertaken duty.'

They shook hands. The Commissaire thanked Denis

Crawford for his cooperation, complimented him on his French, and expressed the hope that he would return to Paris under happier circumstances.

Denis took Sandy's watch and wedding ring to Diana Vaughan. Then, in his old-fashioned way, he set about a decorous courtship of her. She seemed grateful for his attentions and enjoyed being taken out by him for drives with her children. He arranged for the sale of the Renault and came to her house two evenings a week to coach her little boy in French for his coming examination. On her birthday he sent her red roses.

When a year had gone by since Sandy's death, he could wait no longer. He asked her to marry him.

'Oh, my dear,' she said with a little laugh that was only a shade less derisive than Sandy's, 'didn't you know? I thought everyone knew by now. I'm engaged to Malcolm Shaw. I don't suppose it matters your knowing, but we were lovers for ever so long before Sandy died. We're getting married next month.'

Denis Crawford put 500 francs on the table. 'Buy yourself a wedding present,' he said, and he walked out of the house.

The Price of Joy

Daniel Derbyshire had once seen a cartoon in which a thug held a woman captive and bound while his henchman, on the telephone for a ransom, was remarking, 'Her husband don't answer. There's just hysterical laughter.' For a while he kept the newspaper in which it appeared and thought of cutting out the cartoon and pinning it to his office wall. But it was in deplorable taste, so he threw it away.

He was fifty and rich. The newspapers, when they mentioned him, referred to him as a tycoon. In the past they had been in the habit of mentioning him quite often, for his successes, for his business coups, and for the fact that he had been married four times. His first wife was named Joy. She was the mother of his children, and he had been happy with her until a crescendo of success, building up fast but not too fast for him to cope with it, altered his style of living and made Joy appear to him as suburban and commonplace.

At his request she had divorced him so that he could marry

Vivien, who in her turn had divorced him so that he could marry Jane. In common with Henry the Eighth, he had had one wife who had set him free by dying before he could rid himself of her, and his Jane, like Henry's, had died. After her death, when he was 45, he had married Prunella.

At the age they had been – she was six years his junior – men and women are supposed to know their own minds. At last, he thought, he had found someone with whom he could settle down comfortably for the remainder of his life. But her dullness, when the first flush of sexual novelty was over, had nearly driven him mad. What, he sometimes wondered, in her education and her experience, had led her to believe that a man of his sort worth five million wanted love in a cottage, with cosy, suffocating evenings at home, a quiet society-shirking life? It never occurred to him to answer that it was he who had led her to believe it.

And then he met Joy again.

Of course, they had never entirely lost touch. The upbringing of their children, of whom she'd had custody, had seen to that. But for years they had communicated with each other mostly through their lawyers and by way of messages carried from one to the other by their now grown-up children. Five years after his fourth marriage he met Joy at a party, quite by chance.

It was remarkable what the years had done. As a girl, Joy had been rather plain. At fifty-two she was statuesque, elegant, her carefully dressed silver hair surmounting a face that was handsome, wise and sardonic. The alimony she'd had from him had enabled her to travel and buy a mews house in Mayfair. She had met many men, though she had never remarried.

Joy, when young, had never been desired by any man but

himself, but now she was surrounded by men – as he learned when he telephoned her as, these days, he often did. And then, after asking him how he was, she would tell him to hold on for a moment, and he would hear her whisper, 'Oh, Philip, bring me an ashtray, would you?' or 'That's the front doorbell, John. Be an angel and see to it, my dear.'

Her attraction for others made her even more attractive to him. He wanted her again. He saw, in what he observed of her lifestyle and her manners and her dress, that she would be a perfect hostess for him, entertaining his friends as Prunella never could.

He wanted her apart from that. Those children of his would have stared in disbelief had they known with what youthful lust he wanted her, as if they had never made love all those years ago, and he had never grown weary of her.

'You really want to marry me again, Dan?'

'You know I do,' he said. 'We should never have separated.'

'It was you who separated us. You broke my heart.'

'They say it's never too late to mend, Joy. Let me mend it.'

'And what,' said Joy, 'about Prunella?'

One can get used to anything, and Daniel was used to discarding wives. The cumbersome and frightening machinery of the law which keeps many ill-matched couples together, the crippling payments demanded, held no fear for him. 'That won't last, anyway,' he said. 'I'll get a quiet divorce fixed up, one of those incompatibility jobs.'

'Not on my account, you won't,' said Joy. 'Maybe Vivien didn't care about me when she got hold of you, but I'm thirty years older than she was and I do care. I like Prunella, what I've seen of her, and I won't do to her what Vivien did to me.'

'Are you saying you don't want to marry me?'

'No. I'd like to marry you again. I'm still very fond of you, Dan. If Prunella were in love with someone else and left you, that would be a different story.'

'Or if she were to die, I suppose?'

'Of course. But don't have any ideas about getting rid of her, please. I wouldn't put it past you. You're always quite ruthless about getting what you want, and then when you've got it you don't want it any more.'

Daniel, however, hadn't the remotest notion of murdering his wife, and Joy's suggestion slightly shocked him. But those failings in Prunella which had always irritated him now fanned his exasperation to fever pitch. He was more than ever impatient with her timidity which made her shy of appearing with him at distinguished functions, frightened to drive her own car in London, and unwilling to make the simple speech required of her when asked to open the fête in the village where they had their weekend home.

He was nearly enraged when she refused an invitation for them to join a party on a peer's yacht on the grounds that they liked to spend their holidays alone together and quietly in the country. And it was particularly annoying that at this time there appeared in a Sunday-paper supplement an effusive feature about his private life, with many coloured photographs of himself and Prunella in tweeds, himself and Prunella with bounding dogs, himself and Prunella confronting each other tenderly against the background of a log fire.

The captions and text were even worse. Had he really said those things? Had he truly told that reporter that he had come home to port after a long voyage on stormy seas? Had he claimed to have found the Right Woman at last after so much trial and error? He was obliged to admit that he had. But those feature stories take so long to appear, and he had said all those embarrassing things long before he had re-encountered Joy.

The idea that Prunella might fall in love with someone else and leave him — that was an attractive idea. But he was too hard-headed and too much of a realist to hope seriously for it. Prunella was eight years younger than Joy, in his eyes she looked older. And she never met any men except the happily married José who, with his wife, kept house for them, and the elder driver of the minicab she employed whenever she wanted to cross London to visit her mother. (How profoundly this annoyed Daniel, that she should be driven about in a car belonging to a shabby minicab company, when she could have used his Rolls-Royce and his chauffeur.)

Moreover, despite her total lack of dress sense, her preference for costume jewelry over diamonds and her taste for drinking sparkling champagne cider, Prunella was fond of money. She liked spending it on her mother, her sisters and her scruffy nephews and nieces. She had a horse, eating its head off and growing fat in the country. The dogs alone — and they were her dogs — cost a thousand pounds a year in food and veterinary care.

If she left him for another man, he would, of course, contribute something toward her support, but that something would be nothing to what she could skin him for if he left her. And she knew it. She had the examples of Joy's and Vivien's alimony before her.

So Daniel did nothing — that is, he did nothing positive. His negative actions took the form of neglecting Prunella thoroughly, seldom going home before midnight and phoning Joy every day. He saw Joy whenever she allowed him to, but that wasn't often.

'I lead such a hectic life, darling,' she said on the phone. 'For instance, there's Max's private viewing tonight, and naturally I shall be at the première of Ivan's film tomorrow – hold on a moment, would you? Be an angel and get me a drink, David – I'd like to see you, Dan, but really it's so difficult.'

'It wouldn't be so difficult if you wanted to,' growled Daniel, whose desires were greatly inflamed by all these references to the glossy living in which his wife was taking part, and taking part, no doubt, with grace.

'Not much use wanting, is there, Dan? – thank you, David, that's delicious – I'm afraid you've made your bed, my dear, and you must lie on it. With Prunella.'

When they did meet she was affectionate and charming. But, no she wouldn't have an affair with him. It was marriage or nothing, and she had to admit that, at her age, she did rather incline to the companionship and security of marriage.

'But we can be friends,' she said sweetly, adding that things between him and Prunella couldn't be that bad. She too had seen the Sunday supplement in which they looked so cosy and contented with each other. 'And they say the camera doesn't lie, Dan dear.'

Things went on in this way for another six months. Daniel hung about after Joy like a lovesick adolescent, and Prunella took to spending two or three nights a week at her mother's. Then, one Monday lunchtime, he received a telephone call at work. His secretary was temporarily out of the room, and he took the call himself.

A man's voice said, 'We have your wife.'

'I beg your pardon?' said Daniel.

'You heard. We have your wife. There've been enough kidnappings lately for me not to have to spell it out. She's quite safe and nothing'll happen to her – if you pay up.'

'I shall go straight to the police,' said Daniel.

'Don't be so stupid. Good God, I'd have thought a bloke who's made your kind of money'd have had a bit more brains. Don't you read the papers? Haven't you ever read a thriller? You go to the police and we shall know. The moment the police get word of this I'll chop off your wife's right hand and send it to you by first-class mail.'

'You must be mad.'

'I'll call you at home. Seven sharp. You'd better be there.' The phone went dead.

Daniel sent for his secretary, told her he was feeling unwell, and to cancel the conference scheduled for that afternoon. His chauffeur drove him home. The first thing he did was ask José where Mrs Derbyshire was.

'She left by cab at ten this morning, sir, to see her mother.'

But Prunella's mother hadn't seen her since the previous Friday. Daniel told her some reassuring lie, then phoned the minicab company. The boss answered.

'Jim was to pick her up at ten, you say? Hang on. Did you pick up Mrs Derbyshire this morning, Jim? No? No, he didn't, Mr Derbyshire. The booking was cancelled by phone at nine-thirty.'

The gang, whoever they were, must have known Prunella's movements thoroughly, cancelled her booking, and sent her a substitute of their own. He wondered where they were holding her and what sort of ransom they were going to ask. At 7:00 he found out.

'Hallo again,' said the same voice. 'Sitting comfortably? Good. I suppose you're very fond of your wife, aren't you?'

'Of course I am,' said Daniel.

'Of course you are. As a matter of fact, it was all those pictures of domestic bliss in that rag that gave us the idea.'

Daniel cursed the Sunday supplement. Nothing but trouble had come of it. First it had set Joy against him, and now there was this. 'Get on with it,' he snapped.

'Since you're so fond of your wife, you'd pay anything to get her back, wouldn't you? Mrs Derbyshire has admitted to us – under a little pressure – that you're worth five million. So two hundred and fifty thousand pounds wouldn't be asking too much, now, would it?'

'A quarter of a million?' said Daniel, aghast.

'Five percent of what you've got. You won't even notice it. Like to talk to your wife?'

Before Daniel could reply, Prunella had come on the line.

'Oh, Dan, you will give them what they want, won't you? I'm sorry I told them you were so rich, but they made me.'

'Are you all right, Pru?'

'At the moment, but I'm cold and I'm frightened.' She gave a little sob. 'I want to go home. I want to get out of here.' A shriek followed as if someone had stuck a pin in her.

The man came back on.

'A quarter of a million in twenty-pound notes,' he said. 'I quite understand it'll take a day or two to get it. It's Monday now, so we'll say Thursday for delivery date, Thursday evening. You can go to your stockbroker in the morning. Go, not phone. We'll have his premises under observation. If you don't go, I'll send you your wife's left little toe in a matchbox. Call you tomorrow, two o'clock. Okay?'

A couple of sleeping pills afforded Daniel a night's rest. He went into the office as usual. Naturally, he must phone the police – it was a citizen's duty to do that, however unpleasant the consequences. If everyone in this kind of trouble went straight to the police, there would be less of this kidnapping nonsense.

On the other hand, the idea of Prunella's being mutilated wasn't agreeable to think of. She had nice hands, though he was obliged to confess he couldn't remember what her toes looked like. His stockbroker would think it very odd to sell shares at this time amounting to £250,000. Presumably, his bank would have to be notified in advance, as they certainly wouldn't have a quarter of a million lying about in twenty-pound notes. By two o'clock he hadn't phoned the police or been to see his stockbroker. The phone rang.

'You didn't go,' the voice said, and there came the sound of a woman's scream. Daniel shuddered. He thought of that horrible cartoon which wasn't at all true to life.

'You damn –' he began. 'You lowdown filthy swine.'

'There's no need to be rude. If her toe doesn't come in the morning, blame the post office. They've not been too reliable lately. Go to your stockbroker. Now.'

Daniel went. His stockbroker told him it was a very bad time to sell, and wouldn't Mr Derbyshire reconsider? Sure that the scream he had heard was made by Prunella while in the process of having her toe amputated, Daniel said no, he wouldn't reconsider. Back home, he drank a lot of brandy. He thought of phoning Joy, and then thought better of it. He told José that Prunella was staying with her mother, and he told her mother that Prunella had gone to the country.

The next two days were extremely unpleasant. The man phoned four times, but Daniel wasn't allowed to speak to Prunella, who, he was told, was 'feeling too unwell.' On Thursday morning the man said, 'You'll be collecting the cash today, right? Put it in a suitcase, and at seven sharp take the suitcase to Charing Cross Station. Leave it there in a left-luggage locker, and this is what you're to do with the key. Take it into the Embankment Gardens and push it into the earth on the left-hand side of the statue of Sir Arthur Sullivan. Got that? The statue's the one of the old boy with this woman crying and draping herself about. Muse of music or something. As a matter of fact, she reminds me of your wife. Especially at this moment. If you take the police with you or don't bring the cash, I won't be back here by eight-thirty. And if I'm not back here by eight-thirty, we cut Mrs Derbyshire's throat. She's had some experience of the knife already, and she doesn't like it.'

Trembling, Daniel took the morning papers which his secretary handed him. On the front page of the top one was a photograph of Princess Anne at a charity performance of *Firebird*, and in the background could be seen Joy, holding the arm of a tall handsome man. He let out a groan.

'Are you all right, Mr Derbyshire?' his secretary asked.

'Yes – that is, no. Never mind. Call me a cab, will you? I have to go to my bank.'

The bank provided him with a guard to escort him and his large suitcase back to the Derbyshire Building. Daniel put the suitcase under his desk and stared at it. A quarter of a million. What a price to pay for a woman you don't even want! He had intended, within the next few months, to settle just this amount on his son and the same amount on his daughter. That, now, would be impossible. And they might kill Prunella anyway. It would be a fine thing to lose the money and Prunella.

On the other hand, wouldn't it literally be a *fine* thing? Daniel didn't think it would bother him so much to rob his children of part of their patrimony if by parting with that money he could rid himself of Prunella for good.

Immediately he castigated himself for the thought. But it kept returning. What a pity the kidnappers didn't have a keener insight, and had said instead that for a quarter of a million they would kill his wife ... He must be overwrought, he thought, his mind unhinged by all this anxiety.

Five o'clock. He sent his secretary home and then he opened the large suitcase. The notes were new and crisp and pale lilac in colour – 12,500 of them in packets. It was a great deal of money, a queen's ransom. But he would willingly and happily have parted with it if it could have bought him Joy. Instead, it was going to buy him Prunella.

At this point a terrible thought came to Daniel. Until now he had considered going to the police, considered stalling, but he had never considered simply *not paying*. And yet what a fool he was to think it would have been preferable if the man had asked for money to kill her rather than to save her! To kill her need cost him nothing. All he had to do was not pay. Wasn't this, in fact, the answer to the dilemma by which he had been beset for nearly a year?

But poor Prunella, frightened, lonely, cold, maltreated. She was his wife, and once he had loved her. He owed it to her to try to save her. Having closed the suitcase, he sent for his chauffeur and went home.

'Don't put the car away, George. I shall need you again at six-thirty.'

He took the suitcase into his study. Prunella would be back with him by – when? Ten? Midnight? Without, very likely, one of her toes. Still, that hadn't been his fault. Not really. It was disagreeable to think of anyone being killed by having her throat cut. But was there any agreeable way of being killed?

Suicide was a different matter. Obviously it would be preferable to kill oneself with pills and liquor rather than by hanging. But if one were going to be killed, there seemed very little to choose between being strangled or blindfolded and shot or run over by a car. There wasn't a nice way of dying by someone else's violence.

They would kill her anyway, he thought. They wouldn't dare take the risk of her later being able to identify them. And he would have thrown that quarter of a million away just as effectively as if he had sunk it in the Thames. Besides, there was always the chance they wouldn't kill her and the money be lost anyway.

At 6:15 he had another look inside the suitcase. Already, by what he had done, he had lost a couple of days' interest on that money. They would kill Prunella and dump her body by some roadside. The police would see that he'd had the money ready and realize that the gang had killed his wife before he'd had time to pay the ransom. The British public would sympathize with him and understand when, in his grief, he tried to heal his broken heart by remarrying his first wife, the mother of his children.

Six-thirty. The Rolls-Royce stood waiting on the driveway.

Daniel poured himself a large brandy. He waited till 6:40 and then rang the bell for his chauffeur.

'Put the car away, George. I won't be needing it again tonight.'

José served him his solitary dinner at 7:15. Daniel took one mouthful of soup, gagged and rushed to the bathroom where he was sick.

The man phoned at 9:00. Prunella was still alive, minus a hand and a toe. It wasn't very nice for her because they couldn't, under the circumstances, call a doctor to attend her.

The man said, 'Follow the prescribed procedure at nine in the morning, Charing Cross Station and the locker key in the earth by the Sullivan statue.'

Daniel didn't sleep at all. He kept throwing up all night, but he didn't take the suitcase to the station in the morning.

All that day there was no sign from the kidnappers. Late that evening the man phoned again. Daniel put the receiver down without speaking, and after that there were no more calls. His body had begun to twitch and jerk, sweat kept breaking out all over him, and his heartbeat was irregular, sometimes pounding and sometimes seeming to stop altogether in a very frightening way.

But on Saturday morning a great peace descended on him. It was over now, it must be. Prunella was dead, and after a decent interval he could go to Joy, a free, ardent wooer.

No work today. Having made up his mind to get in touch with the police during the next few hours – it would be a bit ticklish, thinking of the right things to say – he took Prunella's two Great Danes and the Dalmatian out for a walk. When he got back he went straight into the study to plan his phone tactics with the police. The large suitcase was open on the desk, and Prunella was standing over it, examining its contents.

He felt himself turn white. He felt as if all the blood had rushed out of his tissues and charged into his heart to start up that hideous pounding once more.

'Thank God you're all right,' he managed to whisper.

She faced him. She looked extremely well, though somewhat disgruntled. It was plain she had all her fingers and toes intact.

'What did you get the money for if you weren't going to pay up?'

'I was,' said Daniel. 'I was stalling.'

'Like hell. You can come in now, Jim.' Prunella opened the door to admit the minicab driver who looked much younger and far more strapping than Daniel remembered him. 'Jim, this is my loving husband,' she said. 'Funny, I ought to have known it wouldn't work.'

Daniel sat down. 'Be kind enough to explain,' he said icily.

'I've been in love with Jim for the past six months, but I knew I wouldn't get much out of you if I left you. And Jim's only got his minicab. So we figured this out. Sorry, Jim, I'm afraid this is it. He doesn't think I'm worth a quarter of a million, so I'll have to stay with him.'

'Stay!' Daniel shouted. 'I wouldn't have you here after what you've done for twice what's in that suitcase! Of all the filthy cruel tricks to play on anyone! You don't know what I've been through. This has probably caused permanent injury to my health. I've lost hundreds in interest on that money.' He was choking with rage. 'I'll divorce you and name that crook, and God help me, I won't give you a damned penny!'

'You haven't any proof,' said Prunella, 'and we won't give you any. From what José says, you've told everyone I've been with mother.' She sighed. 'Jim and I know when we're beaten. We shall part here and now forever.'

'What were you going to do?' Daniel growled.

'Well, since you ask, Jim would have hung onto the cash, and after the fuss had died down I'd have left you and joined him. But that's out of the question now. It won't be very nice for me living with a man who doesn't care if I get my throat cut, but I haven't any choice.' Prunella took her coat off. 'And now I'd better see what José is doing about lunch. I'll try and be a better wife to you now, Dan, to make up for all the trouble I've caused. I won't go out so much and we'll stay in every evening together.'

'You're crazy,' said Daniel. 'I won't stand for it. I'll leave you.' But he couldn't. Joy wouldn't have him if he left her. He jumped up. 'Don't you understand I don't want you!'

'Only too well,' said Prunella, glancing at the suitcase, 'but we'll get over that. We'll work at our marriage, we must. Goodbye, Jim. It was a fine idea while it lasted.'

Daniel seized the suitcase, frantically fastening its clasps. 'Take it,' he shouted. 'Take it and go.'

'D'you mean that?' said the voice of the man on the phone. Jim grinned broadly. 'Thanks a lot.'

'Thank you, Dan. That's very generous of you. And just one other thing. May I take the dogs too?'

'Take what you like and get out of my house!'

He watched them go off down the street together, Jim carrying the quarter of a million in the suitcase, Prunella, one arm linked with his, the other holding the dogs on their triple leash. A large brandy steadied him. No one would believe that a man's own wife could do a thing like that. Of all the bare-faced abominable treachery! And those disgusting threats of mutilation while, no doubt, she'd been laughing in the background, God, how he'd have liked to smash them both! All he hoped now was that they'd get mugged, maimed for life, for the contents of that suitcase.

And then, as his rage cooled into seething resentment, he realized what had been achieved. He was free. Prunella had left him of her own accord. Within three or four months he could be divorced. He rang for George, got into the car, and told George to drive him to a certain mews in Mayfair.

Leaning back against the cushions, he thought of the price he had paid for Joy. Surely no woman of fifty-two, once discarded, had ever before been purchased for a quarter of a million? One day he would tell her. When they were married. But she was worth it. He longed for her with the passion of a boy of twenty, though when he was twenty and courting her for the first time, he had never felt this yearning and this tremulous urgency.

Thirty years ago he had gone to her in her father's house on his old motorbike; now he was going to her in a Rolls-Royce Silver Cloud, having paid a fortune for the privilege of asking her once more to be his wife. His heart raced. He ran up the steps of her house and rang the bell.

She opened the door herself. Daniel thought she looked twenty years younger, perhaps thirty years, yet far more lovely than when he had first seen her. Her silver hair was an anachronism above that youthful flushed face.

'Dan! How lovely. How nice of you to come.'

She turned and led him into the living room before he could take her in his arms. There was a man standing by the table. Strange men kept appearing in his life today, but this one wasn't hiding. He was pouring champagne. Daniel observed vaguely that there were other people there too – strange people getting in his way on this day of all days.

He recognized the champagne pourer as Joy's escort in the newspaper photograph. She must get rid of him and all the others, he thought, and he turned to her impulsively, arrogantly. She smiled and took his arm.

'Dan dear,' she said, 'I want you to meet Paul. We were married this morning.'

The Irony of Hate

I murdered Brenda Goring for what I suppose is the most unusual of motives. She came between me and my wife. By that I don't mean to say that there was anything abnormal in their relationship. They were merely close friends, though 'merely' is hardly the word to use in connection with a relationship which alienates and excludes a once-loved husband. I murdered her to get my wife to myself once more, but instead I have parted us perhaps for ever, and I await with dread, with impotent panic, with the most awful helplessness I have ever known, the coming trial.

By setting down the facts – and the irony, the awful irony that runs through them like a sharp glittering thread – I may come to see things more clearly. I may find some way to convince those inexorable powers that be of how it really was; to make Defending Counsel believe me and not raise his eyebrows and shake his head; to ensure, at any rate, that if Laura and I must be separated she will know as she sees me taken from the court to my long imprisonment, that the truth is known and justice done.

Alone here with nothing else to do, with nothing to wait for but that trial, I could write reams about the character, the appearance, the neuroses, of Brenda Goring. I could write the great hate novel of all time. In this context, though, much of it would be irrelevant, and I shall be as brief as I can.

Some character in Shakespeare says of a woman, 'Would I had never seen her!' And the reply is: 'Then you would have left unseen a very wonderful piece of work.' Well, would indeed I had never seen Brenda. As for her being a wonderful piece of work, I suppose I would agree with that too. Once she had had a husband. To be rid of her for ever, no doubt, he paid her enormous alimony and had settled on her a lump sum with which she bought the cottage up the lane from our house. On our village she made the impact one would expect of such a newcomer. Wonderful she was, an amazing refreshment to all those retired couples and cautious weekenders, with her clothes, her long blonde hair, her sports car, her talents and her jet-set past. For a while, that is. Until she got too much for them to take.

From the first she fastened on to Laura. Understandable in a way, since my wife was the only woman in the locality who was of comparable age, who lived there all the time and who had no job. But surely – or so I thought at first – she would never have singled out Laura if she had had a wider choice. To me my wife is lovely, all I could ever want, the only woman I have ever really cared for, but I know that to others she appears shy, colourless, a simple and quiet little housewife. What, then, had she to offer to that extrovert, that bright bejewelled butterfly? She gave me the beginning of the answer herself.

'Haven't you noticed the way people are starting to shun her, darling? The Goldsmiths didn't ask her to their party last week and Mary Williamson refuses to have her on the fête committee.'

'I can't say I'm surprised,' I said. 'The way she talks and the things she talks about.'

'You mean her love affairs and all that sort of thing? But, darling, she's lived in the sort of society where that's quite normal. It's natural for her to talk like that, it's just that she's open and honest.'

'She's not living in that sort of society now,' I said, 'and she'll have to adapt if she wants to be accepted. Did you notice Isabel Goldsmith's face when Brenda told that story about going off for a weekend with some chap she'd picked up in a bar? I tried to stop her going on about all the men her husband named in his divorce action, but I couldn't. And then she's always saying, "When I was living with so-and-so" and "That was the time of my affair with what's-his-name." Elderly people find that a bit upsetting, you know.'

'Well, we're not elderly,' said Laura, 'and I hope we can be a bit more broad-minded. You do like her, don't you?'

I was always very gentle with my wife. The daughter of clever domineering parents who belittled her, she grew up with an ineradicable sense of her own inferiority. She is a born victim, an inviter of bullying, and therefore I have tried never to bully her, never even to cross her. So all I said was that Brenda was all right and that I was glad, since I was out all day, that she had found a friend and companion of her own age.

And if Brenda had befriended and companioned her only during the day, I daresay I shouldn't have objected. I should have got used to the knowledge that Laura was listening, day in and day out, to stories of a world she had never known, to hearing illicit sex and duplicity glorified, and I should have been safe in the conviction that she was incorruptible. But I had to put up with Brenda myself in the evenings when I got home from my long commuting. There she would be, lounging on our sofa, in her silk trousers or long skirt and high boots, chain-smoking. Or she would arrive with a bottle of wine just as we had sat down to dinner and involve us in one of those favourite debates of hers on the lines of 'Is marriage a dying institution?' or 'Are parents necessary?' And to illustrate some specious point of hers she would come out with some personal experience of the kind that had so upset our elderly friends.

Of course I was not obliged to stay with them. Ours is quite a big house, and I could go off into the dining room or the room Laura called my study. But all I wanted was what I had once had, to be alone in the evenings with my wife. And it was even worse when we were summoned to coffee or drinks with Brenda, there in her lavishly furnished, over-ornate cottage to be shown the latest thing she had made – she was always embroidering and weaving and potting and messing about with watercolours – and shown too the gifts she had received at some time or another from Mark and Larry and Paul and all the dozens of other men there had been in her life. When I refused to go Laura would become nervous and depressed, then pathetically elated if, after a couple of blissful Brenda-less evenings, I suggested for the sake of pleasing her that I supposed we might as well drop in on old Brenda.

What sustained me was the certainty that sooner or later any woman so apparently popular with the opposite sex would find herself a boyfriend and have less or no time for my wife. I couldn't understand why this hadn't happened already and I said so to Laura.

'She does see her men friends when she goes up to London,' said my wife.

'She never has any of them down here,' I said, and that evening when Brenda was treating us to a highly coloured account of some painter she knew called Laszlo who was terribly attractive and who adored her, I said I'd like to meet him and why didn't she invite him down for the weekend?

Brenda flashed her long green-painted fingernails about and gave Laura a conspiratorial woman-to-woman look. 'And what would all the old fuddy-duddies have to say about that, I wonder?'

'Surely you can rise above all that sort of thing, Brenda,' I said.

'Of course I can. Give them something to talk about. I'm quite well aware it's only sour grapes. I'd have Laszlo here like a shot, only he wouldn't come. He hates the country, he'd be bored stiff.'

Apparently Richard and Jonathan and Stephen also hated the country or would be bored or couldn't spare the time. It was much better for Brenda to go up and see them in town, and I noticed that after my probing about Laszlo, Brenda seemed to go to London more often and that the tales of her escapades after these visits became more and more sensational. I think I am quite a perceptive man and soon there began to form in my mind an idea so fantastic that for a while I refused to admit it even to myself. But I put it to the test. Instead of just listening to Brenda and throwing in the occasional rather sour rejoinder, I started asking her questions. I took her up on names and dates. 'I thought you said you met Mark in America?' I would say, or 'But surely you didn't have that holiday with Richard until after your divorce?' I tied her up in knots without her realizing it, and the idea began to seem not so fantastic after all. The final test came at Christmas.

I had noticed that Brenda was a very different woman when she was alone with me than when Laura was with us. If, for example, Laura was out in the kitchen making coffee or, as sometimes happened at the weekends, Brenda dropped in when Laura was out, she was rather cool and shy with me. Gone then were the flamboyant gestures and the provocative remarks, and Brenda would chat about village matters as mundanely as Isabel Goldsmith. Not quite the behaviour one would expect from a self-styled Messalina alone with a young and reasonably personable man. It struck me then that in the days when Brenda had been invited to village parties, and now when she still met neighbours at our parties, she never once attempted a flirtation. Were all the men too old for her to bother with? Was a slim, handsome man of going on fifty too ancient to be considered fair game for a woman who would never see thirty again? Of course they were all married, but so were her Paul and her Stephen, and, if she were to be believed, she had had no compunction about taking them away from their wives.

If she were to be believed. That was the crux of it. Not one of them wanted to spend Christmas with her. No London lover invited her to a party or offered to take her away. She would be with us, of course, for Christmas lunch, for the whole of the day, and at our Boxing Day gathering of friends and relatives. I had hung a bunch of mistletoe in our hall, and on Christmas morning I admitted her to the house myself, Laura being busy in the kitchen.

'Merry Christmas,' I said. 'Give us a kiss, Brenda,' and I took her in my arms under that mistletoe and kissed her on the mouth.

She stiffened. I swear a shudder ran through her. She was as awkward, as apprehensive, as repelled as a sheltered twelve-year-old. And then I knew. Married she may have been – and it was not hard now to guess the cause of her divorce – but she had never had a lover or enjoyed an embrace or even been alone with a man longer than she could help. She was frigid. A good-looking, vivacious, healthy girl, she nevertheless had that particular disability. She was as cold as a nun. But because she couldn't bear the humiliation of admitting it, she had created for herself a fantasy life, a fantasy past, in which she queened it as a fantasy nymphomaniac.

At first I thought it a huge joke and I couldn't wait to tell Laura. But I wasn't alone with her till two in the morning and then she was asleep when I came to bed. I didn't sleep much. My elation dwindled as I realized I hadn't any real proof and that if I told Laura what I'd been up to, probing and questioning and testing, she would only be bitterly hurt and resentful. How could I tell her I'd kissed her best friend and got an icy response? That, in her absence, I'd tried flirting with her best friend and been repulsed? And then, as I thought about it, I understood what I really had discovered, that Brenda hated men, that no man would ever come and take her away or marry her and live here with her and absorb all her time. For ever she would stay here alone, living a stone's throw from us, in and out of our house daily, she and Laura growing old together.

I could have moved house, of course. I could have taken Laura away. From her friends? From the house and the countryside she loved? And what guarantee would I have had that Brenda wouldn't have moved too to be near us still? For I knew now what Brenda saw in my wife, a gullible innocent, a trusting everlastingly credulous audience whose own inexperience kept her from seeing the holes and discrepancies in those farragos of nonsense and whose pathetic determination to be worldly prevented her from showing distaste. As the dawn came and I looked with love and sorrow at Laura sleeping beside me, I knew what I must do, the only thing I could do. At the season of peace and goodwill, I decided to kill Brenda Goring for my own and Laura's good and peace.

Easier decided than done. I was buoyed up and strengthened by knowing that in everyone's eyes I would have no motive. Our neighbours thought us wonderfully charitable and tolerant to put up with Brenda at all. I resolved to be positively nice to her instead of just negatively easygoing, and as the New Year came in I took to dropping in on Brenda on my way back from the post or the village shop, and if I got home from work to find Laura alone I asked where Brenda was and suggested we should phone her at once and ask her to dinner or for a drink. This pleased Laura enormously.

'I always felt you didn't really like Brenda, darling,' she said, 'and it made me feel rather guilty. It's marvellous that you're beginning to see how nice she really is.'

What I was actually beginning to see was how I could kill her and get away with it, for something happened which seemed to deliver her into my hands. On the outskirts of the village, in an isolated cottage, lived an elderly unmarried woman called Peggy Daley, and during the last week of January the cottage was broken into and Peggy stabbed to death with her own kitchen knife. The work of some psychopath, the police seemed to believe, for nothing had been stolen or damaged. When it appeared likely that they weren't going to find the killer, I began thinking of how I could kill Brenda in the same way so that the killing could look like the work of the same perpetrator. Just as I was working this out Laura went down with a flu bug she caught from Mary Williamson.

Brenda, of course, came in to nurse her, cooked my dinner for me and cleaned the house. Because everyone believed that Peggy Daley's murderer was still stalking the village, I walked Brenda home at night, even though her cottage was only a few yards up the lane or narrow path that skirted the end of our garden. It was pitch dark there as we had all strenuously opposed the installation of street lighting, and it brought me an ironical amusement to notice how Brenda flinched and recoiled when on these occasions I made her take my arm. I always made a point of going into the house with her and putting all the lights on. When Laura began to get better and all she wanted in the evenings was to sleep I sometimes went earlier to Brenda's, had a nightcap with her, and once, on leaving, I gave her a comradely kiss on the doorstep to show any observing neighbour what friends we were and how much I appreciated all Brenda's kindness to my sick wife.

Then I got the flu myself. At first this seemed to upset my plans, for I couldn't afford to delay too long. Already people were beginning to be less apprehensive about our marauding murderer and were getting back to their old habits of leaving their back doors unlocked. But then I saw how I could turn my illness to my advantage. On the Monday, when I had been confined to bed for three days and that ministering angel Brenda was fussing about me nearly as much as my own wife was, Laura remarked that she wouldn't go across to the Goldsmiths that evening as she had promised because it seemed wrong to leave me. Instead, if I was better by then, she would go on the Wednesday, her purpose being to help Isabel cut out a dress. Brenda, of course, might have offered to stay with me instead, and I think Laura was a little surprised that she didn't. I knew the reason and had a little quiet laugh to myself about it. It was one thing for Brenda to flaunt about, regaling us with stories of all the men she had nursed in the past, quite another to find herself alone with a not very sick man in that man's bedroom.

So I had to be sick enough to provide myself with an alibi but not sick enough to keep Laura at home. On the Wednesday morning I was feeling a good deal better. Dr Lawson looked in on his way back from his rounds in the afternoon and pronounced, after a thorough examination, that I still had phlegm on my chest. While he was in the bathroom washing his hands and doing something with his stethoscope, I held the thermometer he had stuck in my mouth against the radiator at the back of the bed. This worked better than I had hoped, worked, in fact, almost too well. The mercury went up to a hundred and three, and I played up to it by saying in a feeble voice that I felt dizzy and kept alternating between the sweats and the shivers.

'Keep him in bed,' Dr Lawson said, 'and give him plenty of warm drinks. I doubt if he could get up if he tried.'

I said rather shamefacedly that I had tried and I couldn't and that my legs felt like jelly. Immediately Laura said she wouldn't go out that night, and I blessed Lawson when he told her not to be silly. All I needed was rest and to be allowed to sleep. After a good deal of fussing and self-reproach and promises not to be gone more than two hours at the most, she finally went off at seven.

As soon as the car had departed, I got up. Brenda's house could be seen from my bedroom window, and I saw that she had lights on but no porch light. The night was dark, moonless and starless. I put trousers and a sweater on over my pyjamas and made my way downstairs.

By the time I was halfway down I knew that I needn't have

pretended to be ill or bothered with the thermometer ploy. I *was* ill. I was shivering and swaying, great waves of dizziness kept coming over me, and I had to hang on to the banisters for support. That wasn't the only thing that had gone wrong. I had intended, when the deed was done and I was back home again, to cut up my coat and gloves with Laura's electric scissors and burn the pieces on our living-room fire. But I couldn't find the scissors and I realized Laura must have taken them with her to her dressmaking session. Worse than that, there was no fire alight. Our central heating was very efficient and we only had an open fire for the pleasure and cosiness of it, but Laura hadn't troubled to light one while I was upstairs ill. At that moment I nearly gave up. But it was then or never. I would never again have such circumstances and such an alibi. Either kill her now, I thought, or live in an odious *ménage à trois* for the rest of my life.

We kept the raincoats and gloves we used for gardening in a cupboard in the kitchen by the back door. Laura had left only the hall light on, and I didn't think it would be wise to switch on any more. In the semi-darkness I fumbled about in the cupboard for my raincoat, found it and put it on. It seemed tight on me, my body was so stiff and sweaty, but I managed to button it up, and then I put on the gloves. I took with me one of our kitchen knives and let myself out by the back door. It wasn't a frosty night, but raw and cold and damp.

I went down the garden, up the lane and into the garden of Brenda's cottage. I had to feel my way round the side of the house, for there was no light there at all. But the kitchen light was on and the back door unlocked. I tapped and let myself in without waiting to be asked. Brenda, in full evening rig, glittery sweater, gilt necklace, long skirt, was cooking her solitary supper. And then, for the first time ever, when it didn't matter any more, when it was too late, I felt pity for her. There she was, a handsome, rich, gifted woman with the reputation of a seductress, but in reality as destitute of people who really cared for her as poor old Peggy Daley had been; there she was, dressed for a party, heating up tinned spaghetti in a cottage kitchen at the back of beyond.

She turned round, looking apprehensive, but only, I think, because she was always afraid when we were alone that I would try to make love to her.

'What are you doing out of bed?' she said, and then, 'Why are you wearing those clothes?'

I didn't answer her. I stabbed her in the chest again and again. She made no sound but a little choking moan and she crumpled up on the floor. Although I had known how it would be, had hoped for it, the shock was so great and I had already been feeling so swimmy and strange, that all I wanted was to throw myself down too and close my eyes and sleep. That was impossible. I turned off the cooker. I checked that there was no blood on my trousers and my shoes, though of course there was plenty on the raincoat, and then I staggered out, switching off the light behind me.

I don't know how I found my way back, it was so dark and by then I was lightheaded and my heart was drumming. I just had the presence of mind to strip off the raincoat and the gloves and push them into our garden incinerator. In the morning I would have to get up enough strength to burn them before Brenda's body was found. The knife I washed and put back in the drawer.

Laura came back about five minutes after I had got myself to bed. She had been gone less than half an hour. I turned over and managed to raise myself up to ask her why she was back so soon. It seemed to me that she had a strange distraught look about her.

'What's the matter?' I mumbled. 'Were you worried about me?'

'No,' she said, 'no,' but she didn't come up close to me or put her hand on my forehead. 'It was – Isabel Goldsmith told me something – I was upset – I … It's no use talking about it now, you're too ill.' She said in a sharper tone than I had ever heard her use, 'Can I get you anything?'

'I just want to sleep,' I said.

'I shall sleep in the spare room. Good night.'

That was reasonable enough, but we had never slept apart before during the whole of our marriage, and she could hardly have been afraid of catching the flu, having only just got over it herself. But I was in no state to worry about that, and I fell into the troubled nightmare-ridden sleep of fever. I remember one of those dreams. It was of Laura finding Brenda's body herself, a not unlikely eventuality.

However, she didn't find it. Brenda's cleaner did. I knew what must have happened because I saw the police car arrive from my window. An hour or so later Laura came in to tell me the news which she had got from Jack Williamson.

'It must have been the same man who killed Peggy,' she said.

I felt better already. Things were going well. 'My poor darling,' I said, 'you must feel terrible, you were such close friends.'

She said nothing. She straightened my bedclothes and left the room. I knew I should have to get up and burn the contents of the incinerator, but I couldn't get up. I put my feet out and reached for the floor, but it was as if the floor came up to meet me and threw me back again. I wasn't over-worried. The police would think what Laura thought, what everyone must think.

That afternoon they came, a chief inspector and a sergeant. Laura brought them up to our bedroom and they talked to us together. The chief inspector said he understood we were close friends of the dead woman, wanted to know when we had last seen her and what we had been doing on the previous evening. Then he asked if we had any idea at all as to who had killed her.

'That maniac who murdered the other woman, of course,' said Laura.

'I can see you don't read the papers,' he said.

Usually we did. It was my habit to read a morning paper in the office and to bring an evening paper home with me. But I had been at home ill. It turned out that a man had been arrested on the previous morning for the murder of Peggy Daley. The shock made me flinch and I'm sure I turned pale. But the policemen didn't seem to notice. They thanked us for our cooperation, apologized for disturbing a sick man, and left. When they had gone I asked Laura what Isabel had said to upset her the night before. She came up to me and put her arms round me.

'It doesn't matter now,' she said. 'Poor Brenda's dead and it was a horrible way to die, but – well, I must be very wicked – but I'm not sorry. Don't look at me like that, darling. I love you and I know you love me, and we must forget her and be as we used to be. You know what I mean.'

I didn't, but I was glad whatever it was had blown over. I had enough on my plate without a coldness between me and my wife. Even though Laura was beside me that night, I hardly slept for worrying about the stuff in that incinerator. In the morning I put up the best show I could of being much better. I dressed and announced, in spite of Laura's expostulations, that I was going into the garden. The police were there already, searching all our gardens, actually digging up Brenda's.

They left me alone that day and the next, but they came in once and interviewed Laura on her own. I asked her what they had said, but she passed it off quite lightly. I supposed she didn't think I was well enough to be told they had been enquiring about my movements and my attitude towards Brenda.

'Just a lot of routine questions, darling,' she said, but I was sure she was afraid for me, and a barrier of her fear for me and mine for myself came up between us. It seems incredible but that Sunday we hardly spoke to each other and when we did Brenda's name wasn't mentioned. In the evening we sat in silence, my arm round Laura, her head on my shoulder, waiting, waiting ...

The morning brought the police with a search warrant. They asked Laura to go into the living room and me to wait in the study. I knew then that it was only a matter of time. They would find the knife, and of course they would find Brenda's blood on it. I had been feeling so ill when I cleaned it that now I could no longer remember whether I had scrubbed it or simply rinsed it under the tap.

After a long while the chief inspector came in alone.

'You told us you were a close friend of Miss Goring's.'

'I was friendly with her,' I said, trying to keep my voice steady. 'She was my wife's friend.'

He took no notice of this. 'You didn't tell us you were on

intimate terms with her, that you were, in point of fact, having a sexual relationship with her.'

Nothing he could have said would have astounded me more.

'That's absolute rubbish!'

'Is it? We have it on sound authority.'

'What authority?' I said. 'Or is that the sort of thing you're not allowed to say?'

'I see no harm in telling you,' he said easily. 'Miss Goring herself informed two women friends of hers in London of the fact. She told one of your neighbours she met at a party in your house. You were seen to spend evenings alone with Miss Goring while your wife was ill, and we have a witness who saw you kissing her good night.'

Now I knew what it was that Isabel Goldsmith had told Laura which had so distressed her. The irony of it, the irony ... Why hadn't I, knowing Brenda's reputation and knowing Brenda's fantasies, suspected what construction would be put on my assumed friendship with her? Here was motive, the lack of which I had relied on as my last resort. Men do kill their mistresses, from jealousy, from frustration, from fear of discovery.

But surely I could turn Brenda's fantasies to my own use?

'She had dozens of men friends, lovers, whatever you like to call them. Any of them could have killed her.'

'On the contrary,' said the chief inspector, 'apart from her ex-husband who is in Australia, we have been able to discover no man in her life but yourself.'

I cried out desperately, 'I didn't kill her! I swear I didn't.'

He looked surprised. 'Oh, we know that.' For the first time he called me sir. 'We know that, sir. No one is accusing you of anything. We have Dr Lawson's word for it that you were physically incapable of leaving your bed that night, and the raincoat and gloves we found in your incinerator are not your property.'

Fumbling in the dark, swaying, the sleeves of the raincoat too short, the shoulders too tight ... 'Why are you wearing those clothes?' she had asked before I stabbed her.

'I want you to try and keep calm, sir,' he said very gently. But I have never been calm since. I have confessed again and again, I have written statements, I have expostulated, raved, gone over with them every detail of what I did that night, I have wept.

Then I said nothing. I could only stare at him. 'I came in here to you, sir,' he said, 'simply to confirm a fact of which we were already certain, and to ask you if you would care to accompany your wife to the police station where she will be charged with the murder of Miss Brenda Goring.'

Digby's Wives

Although our ways afterwards diverged, I was at school with Digby Ambeach and the fact of our having once been school fellows was enough for my mother to feel she had to keep me informed of his doings. 'Digby Ambeach is getting married,' she said when I came home from college at the end of my first term.

'He can't be more than nineteen.'

'There's no harm in settling down young when you know your own mind. Digby's done very well for himself. She's a bit older than he is; she's twenty-one, a judge's daughter, and I hear she came into quite a bit of money of her own on her birthday.'

'How did he work that?' I said. 'A solicitor's clerk?'

'Digby's a very nice-looking young man and a very *nice* young man. I hope you'll see something of him now you're home.'

I said I'd think about it, but I was too busy with a nice-looking young woman to spare any time for Digby Ambeach.

My mother went on giving me snippets of news of him. She wrote to me devotedly every week. One of those letters, about five years later, told me about what she called Digby's tragedy. His wife had been drowned while they were boating on the Norfolk Broads.

I wrote him a letter of condolence. The following Christmas I went home for the holiday and my mother told me Digby had invested all the money his wife had left him as well as the sum for which her life had been insured in house property.

'He's got four houses now, all let off into flats, and he's got a furniture shop in Chelsea.' My mother levelled a disappointed look at me. 'Oh, yes, Digby's done very well. He hasn't wasted his time.'

An old girlfriend of mine lived in Fulham. I was on my way to see her, driving down the King's Road, when I noticed a shop called Ambeach Antiques. It was well down below the World's End and the stuff for sale looked as undistinguished as the neighbourhood.

I went in and Digby came out from a room at the back. We hadn't seen each other for seven years but he treated me like his best friend.

'Welcome to the emporium, sonny boy.' I was later to learn that Digby called all men 'sonny boy' – and all women 'doll'. 'Not exactly Sotheby's, is it? Still, it keeps the wolf from the door.'

'According to my mother,' I said, 'you're a business genius.'

'And, according to *my* mother, you're the Master of Balliol.' With that touch of nature to make us kin, we laughed together. 'I'm glad you dropped in,' he said, 'because I've got a bit of news that hasn't gone out on the maternal network. I'm getting married again next week.'

Thus it was that Olivia came into my life.

Digby must have gathered through what he called the maternal network that I had left my job in the north of England and taken a teaching post in a college of technology a little way outside London, for about six months after our meeting in the antique shop I got an invitation to dine with him and his new wife.

They were living in a flat in one of Digby's rickety old houses in a run-down corner of Maida Vale. It smelled of the canal and it was in urgent need of redecoration, but in the presence of Olivia Ambeach you took no more notice of the walls and ceilings than you would of the jam jar that holds an orchid.

'What do you think of her, sonny boy?' said Digby while his wife was out in the kitchen.

'Gorgeous. Why did no one tell me she was ravishingly beautiful?'

Digby gave me a funny look. 'Yes, she's a pretty girl,' he said, 'and I'm glad to say she hasn't come to me empty-handed. She was a widow, you know. Her late husband's life assurance will come in quite handy, I can tell you.'

He disgusted me. Why had she married him? Why had she thrown herself away on a money-grubbing clod? I asked her those questions myself when we were in bed in a nasty little hotel in Paddington.

'He was so keen to marry me,' she said, 'I just gave in. He thought I'd got more money than I really have.' She laughed. 'And I thought he'd got more than he has.'

'You were the more deceived.'

'He's a cheerful soul,' said Olivia, 'and very even-tempered,' which gave an insight into what her first husband had been like.

'Leave him and come away with me,' I said. All this was some year or so after her marriage and my change of job and I was awaiting confirmation of an academic post in Australia. 'You can't throw your whole life away on Digby Ambeach.'

She gave me one of her enigmatic smiles. 'I don't suppose I shall,' she said, but she wouldn't come with me. Six weeks later we said goodbye and she saw me off at Heathrow.

We had agreed not to correspond. It was my mother who wrote to tell me Olivia had left Digby. 'Disappeared into thin air. No one knows where she has gone, but my belief is she has run off with one of those men who were always hanging round her.' I winced at that. I had got over Olivia but still it hurt to know I hadn't been the only one.

My mother's next letter was a bombshell. Digby had moved into the maternal home and there were suggestions going about – *ugly rumours*, my mother called them – as to the reason for Olivia's disappearance. What could she mean? I wrote back, asking for an explanation; for I imagined the police interrogating Digby and digging up the Maida Vale garden.

An answer came but not the one I wanted. My mother had quarrelled with Mrs Ambeach, who had accused her of spreading slanders about her son, and they were no longer on speaking terms. Reading between the lines, I gathered that my mother had been frightened into never uttering Digby's name, still less setting anything down about him on paper.

For a while, because Olivia and I had been lovers and she was beautiful and I had been in love with her, I thought I ought to do something. I ought to take some kind of action. You see, I remembered that first wife of Digby's, drowned in a boating accident.

She had left him money. Had he persuaded Olivia to put her bit of money into one of his abortive business ventures and then made away with her? I wondered. It was very disquieting.

But twelve thousand miles is a long distance. It makes the heart less fond and home anxieties remote. Gradually I began to tell myself that Olivia would have turned up by now, that she was alive and happy somewhere and all was well.

For ten years I remained in Australia, going home only once in all that time when my mother fell ill. The doctors gave her three months to live but she died in three weeks. Mrs Ambeach, her enmity forgotten, came to the funeral.

'How's Digby?' I asked her after the ceremony.

'He's fine. Did you know he'd got married again?'

No, I hadn't known. There had been a rather aggressive or defiant note in her voice. After a little hesitation, I asked about Olivia.

'Remarried.' She looked daggers at me. 'I don't know any details, you'll have to ask Digby.' I could have done, of course, but I didn't much want to. He might possibly know I had been one of the men who were 'always hanging round' Olivia. She had promised never to tell him. But I know what that sort of promise amounts to when a woman is quarrelling with her husband before leaving him.

I was relieved to know that my fears had been groundless, that there had evidently been a divorce and both parties embarked on fresh matrimonial ventures. There seemed no reason why Digby Ambeach and I should ever meet again.

But we did.

A friend of mine wrote to me from London, offering me a partnership in his now flourishing business. It promised to be more lucrative than my present job and, besides, I was growing tired of the academic life. I flew home to England in the July and set about flat-hunting.

The way rents had risen appalled me. What I had been paying for a whole flat before I went away would now just about get a furnished room. It looked as if I should have to buy a place, but that takes time and I was still a grateful but embarrassed guest in my friend's house when I ran into Digby.

To save my hostess extra burdens I was eating my evening meal in a pub in St. John's Wood when someone came up behind me and gave me a hearty slap on the shoulder. 'Long time no see, sonny boy. When did you get back from Down Under?'

I told him.

'You haven't changed a bit.'

Digby had. His thick brown hair had turned prematurely grey. It gave him a military look. I am no judge of good looks in men but if I were a woman I think I should find Digby handsome. He had lost weight and the grey didn't age him.

He bought us both a drink. 'Where are you living now, sonny boy?'

I told him and told him, too, about my housing problem. He looked interested but he made no particular comment and then, suddenly, to my astonishment, he started talking about Olivia. It was a fact, wasn't it, that I had made inquiries about her through my mother and then through his? Had I heard the police had suspected (his phrase) foul play? I felt very awkward.

'It wasn't an easy time for me,' said Digby. 'But she's married

to a very nice chap now and we all get on like a house on fire.'
He put his head on one side and gave me a slow grinding wink.
'I don't think I'll give you her address, though. You might take
it into your head to break up another of her marriages.' My face
grew hot. 'Digby ...'

'Don't say a word, sonny boy. Bless you, I don't mind any more.
A lot of water has flowed under the bridge since then.' He gave me
another slap on the back. 'I tell you what, I've been thinking: there's
a flat at the top of my house going vacant – bedsit, kitchen and bathroom. Only twenty quid a week, seeing you're an old pal.'

That was about half what I should have had to pay elsewhere for
similar accommodation. I began thanking him.

'Say no more. It's just the place for you. Drink up your drink
and we'll go and have a look at it. You can meet Lily at the same
time.' In the taxi I began wondering about his Lily and speculated
as to whether he had married another young beauty.

As we got out in front of Digby's house, he touched my arm
and said: 'Not a word about Olivia in front of Lily, sonny boy.
She's inclined to be possessive.'

They had the ground floor. Digby took me into a living room at
the back. There was an old woman sitting at a table with the *Financial Times* spread out in front of her, and for a moment I thought it
was Digby's mother. But when she turned, I saw it wasn't.

'My wife, Lily,' said Digby very breezily, 'and this is Michael
Dashwood, doll, an old pal of mine.'

I can't begin to tell how grotesque it was to hear Digby call
her 'doll'. She was twenty-five years older than he and she hadn't
made any effort to look younger than she was. Her hair was white,

her face lined and she wore a mannish navy-blue suit with cigarette ash spilled down the front.

'How do you do?' said Lily without enthusiasm. Digby went away to fetch us all a drink and Lily immediately began talking about money. She talked as if she had known me for years but at the same time as if she took no personal interest in me. The Stock Market was her passion. I gathered that she was well-off and kept a tight rein on her own money.

By the time Digby came back with a bottle of whiskey and three glasses, she had told me the King's Road shop had failed, as had a couple of Digby's other ventures.

'He can't expect any financial backing from me,' she said.

Digby gave her a strained smile. 'Whiskey, doll.'

'No, thanks,' said Lily. 'If you didn't drink so much, you'd have a better head for business.'

Five minutes later she had folded up her newspaper, stuck it under her arm and gone off to bed. It was ten to nine. Digby and I went upstairs to look at the vacant flat. We passed the first floor and the flat on the second floor where he had lived with Olivia, and the third floor that was let off in single rooms and came to a very steep and narrow staircase – a real death trap, I thought. I should have to be very careful of it if I took the place.

The top floor had originally consisted of two very large rooms, the doors to which opened on to a landing. One of them led into a bed-sitting room with kitchen and bathroom off it. It was shabby but quite well-appointed, light and airy and a cinch at twenty pounds.

'Like it?' said Digby.

'Very much.'

'I'll do you proud. I'll have the place painted before you move in. And I'll get you a fridge.'

It wasn't till I got back to my friend's house that an odd discrepancy struck me. They all got on like a house on fire, Digby had said, referring presumably to the amicable relations that prevailed between the Ambeaches and Olivia and her husband. On the other hand, Olivia's name wasn't to be mentioned to Lily because she was jealous. Something was wrong somewhere.

Suppose there was another reason for this prohibition of Olivia's name. Because Lily would have said that she had never in her life set eyes on Olivia? I thought about that a lot and I thought about Digby's first wife, too, the one who had drowned. It made me distinctly uneasy but it didn't stop me moving into the flat at the appointed time.

True to his word, Digby had had the flat redecorated and had got me a fridge.

'I don't like the idea of having it in that alcove,' I said.

'You can't have it in the kitchen,' said Digby. 'The electric point's faulty.'

'Then we'll have it mended. After all, this is my living room and my bedroom. I don't want to sit here looking at a refrigerator.' I went into the kitchen and saw a space between the oven and the sink. 'That's where it can go,' I said, 'and we'll get an electrician in.'

The last thing I expected was for Digby to fly into a rage, but that is exactly what he did. Even-tempered, Olivia had once called him, and I would have described him that way myself. His face went red and his eyes bulged.

'Now look here,' he shouted, 'I don't want you coming here and criticizing my arrangements. I let you have this flat for a measly twenty quid a week and the minute you get in you start nit-picking. I want that fridge where I've put it and I don't want you messing about with the wiring. Be a fine thing, wouldn't it, if you set the place on fire.'

'I shan't do that.'

'Did you hear me say to leave that bloody fridge where it is or did you not?'

By then I was really intrigued. Why should Digby care where I kept the fridge? And why did it excite him so? He looked angry enough to turn me out almost before I had moved in. I didn't want to lose the flat, so I gave in and said I expected I would get used to it.

At once he was his old self again, the 'cheerful soul'. He smiled and patted my shoulder. 'Of course you will, sonny boy. Sorry about that outburst, I get a bit edgy sometimes – money worries, you know.' And off he went back to Lily.

The minute he had gone I tested the point in the kitchen. I plugged in the iron and it functioned perfectly. Then I switched off the electricity in the meter cupboard, took the point off the wall and examined it. There was nothing wrong with it.

Now to move the fridge. Immediately I saw – or thought I saw – the true reason for Digby's bad temper. Whoever had done the wallpapering had botched the job at the bottom of the alcove where he had apparently run out of paper and left about a foot of bare plaster ... or rather, plaster*board*.

I tapped the half-papered panel and it rang hollow. Of course, I thought. Of course. It wasn't really an alcove at all but a doorway and Digby, when constructing this flat, had removed the door which communicated with the other large room and boarded up the space. He wanted to stop me getting into that other room or even knowing there was a way in.

The alcove panel was screwed fairly lightly in place but the last thing I was likely to find was a screwdriver. The funny thing was, though, that when on the off-chance I looked in the drawer under the sink the only object in it happened to be a screwdriver. I never had a very high opinion of Digby's intelligence and now it fell even further.

The man didn't want me to get into that room, yet had fallen into a guilty rage as soon as I showed signs of interest in the alcove and had also left a screwdriver handy for a little breaking and entering.

I was determined to break and enter.

The panel came away easily. On the other side of it was a room about the same size as my whole flat filled with what I knew at once to be the unsaleable contents of the shop Digby used to have in Chelsea: old armchairs with broken seats, wicker tables and brass-topped tables, lithographs in thick frames, incomplete sets of encyclopaedias, a birdcage, Victorian basins and water jugs, medical books, something that might have been an early dentist's drill, and dominating everything, a huge wardrobe with brass handles. I poked about in this lot for a few minutes. It was stuffy in that room and everything was coated with dust, the kind of dust that is not a patina but a fur. I couldn't understand why Digby hadn't wanted me to go in there. Because he didn't want me to see this evidence of his failure? Surely not. He talked freely about his failures.

I stood in front of the wardrobe and stared at it, and something told me that whatever it was Digby didn't want me to find was behind those marble-veined doors.

Leave it, I said to myself, it isn't your business. Old Digby is keeping something grotesque and undignified in there – pornography or objects of fetishism ... But I was already opening the door.

What I saw made me jump backwards and almost fall over the birdcage and the medical books. Hanging in the wardrobe from a hook in the centre of the top of it was a skeleton dressed in the red trouser suit Olivia had worn when she saw me off at Heathrow more than a decade before.

I remembered reading somewhere that it takes about ten years for a corpse to become a skeleton. I imagined Olivia's body – that exquisite body – slowly rotting inside those clothes, the hair falling from her head, the eyes ... At that point I plunged back through the hole in the wall and into my bathroom to be very sick.

Luckily, I had a bottle of brandy with me. I poured myself a stiff measure and then another. My phone hadn't yet been installed so I dashed down the stairs, nearly falling down that steep top flight, and ran hell for leather to the phone box on the corner.

What happened next makes me look all kinds of a fool. The police came, no less than three of them plus a doctor. They hauled Digby out and he was the picture of guilt, protesting that this was an outrage and an infringement of his privacy and what would his friends think? Apparently, a couple of friends had just dropped in to see him and Lily. We all trooped upstairs. I let them into my flat and through the hole in the wall we went.

The detective inspector, whose name was Doyle, opened the

wardrobe. Inside it, all on hangers, were two skirts, two dresses and the red trouser suit.

'But it was there,' I said.

'It isn't there now, sir,' said the inspector.

Digby, looking very grave and solemn, picked his way across the room. There on the floor, somewhat huddled up, lay the skeleton.

'That,' said the doctor, 'is a hundred years old.' He prodded it. If you take a look you can see it's been wired.'

'All this junk,' said Digby, giving me a magnanimous smile, 'comes from a shop I used to have. I inherited the skeleton and the medical books from an ancestor.'

'Not dear old Ambeach of the Royal Free?' said the doctor.

'My great uncle,' said Digby and after that they all got very matey, poking at the skeleton and looking at its teeth, while Digby explained that the clothes in the wardrobe belonged to his former wife and had been left behind when they split up.

Everyone seemed to have forgotten about me until Digby gave me one of his slaps on the back.

'Cheer up, sonny boy,' he said, 'We all make mistakes. Now why don't we all go down for a drink?'

'We're on duty, you know, sir,' said Doyle in a tone that indicated he wouldn't let duty come between him and a drink. His eye gimleted me. 'I should say Mr Dashwood has had quite enough already.'

Lily glared when we all walked in. There were two other people with her, a man and a woman. I heard Doyle say, 'Ah, the skeleton in the cupboard,' as he was introduced to Olivia. Then the floor came up and I passed out.

When I came round, the law had departed and Lily had

disappeared. But Olivia and her husband were still there. She was as beautiful as ever.

'Here she is, in the flesh,' said Digby. 'Make old bones yet, won't you, doll?'

'I can't understand what possessed me,' I said. 'I must have lost my mind.'

Digby couldn't have been nicer about it. He laughed and joked. He told all his friends and all the tenants in the house. In fact, he laboured the point too much, but I hadn't the heart to reproach him after he had been so kind. Everyone in the neighbourhood must have got to know how I had had a hallucination of a skeleton hanging in a cupboard and had accused Digby of murdering his second wife.

Not long after that, he asked me if I would like to buy the flat I was living in – the whole top floor in fact, including what we had all come to call the 'skeleton room' – and the price he named was so modest I didn't hesitate.

'I'm in low water, sonny boy,' he said, 'but those few thousands from you will just about tide me over till something else turns up.'

'Lily can't help?'

'Let's say she won't. It's her money. I daresay it gives her the one pleasure she gets out of life.'

On the day I paid Digby and the flat became mine, I asked him and Lily to come up for a celebration drink. They arrived at seven, Lily looking particularly grumpy, and the Scotch she consumed didn't improve her temper. I suppose she and I put away the best part of half a bottle between us; but Digby stuck to soda water, saying he had nervous indigestion.

As usual, Lily talked about money. She took a gloomy view of the state of sterling. 'Mark my words,' she said, 'we shall all see the pound revalued before we're much older.'

Sound though she was in these matters, she was wrong there. She at any rate will never see it. Suddenly, in her abrupt way, she announced at nine that it was her bedtime and got up to leave us. Digby said he would stay a bit longer. Lily went off and after that – well, I don't think I can do better than to tell you what happened when the police came.

Digby and I hadn't touched Lily's body. It lay in a crumpled heap at the foot of that steep staircase. Somehow or other we both knew she was dead. It was a different doctor that came but the senior officer was Inspector Doyle.

'I heard Mrs Ambeach scream,' I said, 'and then the crash. After that the front door closed and …'

'Do you realize what you're saying, Mr Dashwood?' Doyle leaned towards me, sniffing my breath. 'Do you know what you're implying?'

Digby said gently: 'Mike, sonny boy, who could have closed the door when you and I were sitting in here together?'

But he had gone to the door with Lily, gone outside briefly with Lily … 'I heard her scream and fall and then the door closed …' I stopped and looked at Doyle.

'Be careful what you say, Mr Dashwood. You've had a fair bit of drink. I'd call you a heavy drinker. You must be sure of your facts this time. We haven't forgotten what happened here a couple of months back. Now, when you heard Mrs Ambeach scream and fall, where was Mr Ambeach?''

I couldn't repeat my folly all over again, could I? Accuse Digby a second time and a second time doubtless be proved wrong?

'I'm sorry,' I said. 'I think I have had a bit too much to drink. Mr Ambeach and I were sitting in here. Mrs Ambeach said good night and closed the door and then we heard her scream and fall.'

There was an inquest and the verdict was Accidental Death. Digby was very upset about losing Lily and he didn't even get the consolation he expected. Her investments turned out to be pitifully small. It had been all talk with her.

But since then, things have started looking up for Digby as they usually seem to. He has met a very nice woman, a widow, who runs a flourishing business her husband left her. The only difficulty is that though she is prepared to live with him, so far she has turned down his offers of marriage.

'I expect she'll give in,' Olivia said to me. 'Digby is a great manipulator and he's prepared to go to endless trouble to get what he wants.'

'I suppose he is,' I said.

The Haunting of Shawley Rectory

I don't believe in the supernatural, but just the same I wouldn't live in Shawley Rectory.

That was what I had been thinking and what Gordon Scott said to me when we heard we were to have a new rector at St Mary's. Our wives gave us quizzical looks.

'Not very logical,' said Eleanor, my wife.

'What I mean is,' said Gordon, 'that however certain you might be that ghosts don't exist, if you lived in a place that was reputedly haunted you wouldn't be able to help wondering every time you heard a stair creak. All the normal sounds of an old house would take on a different significance.'

I agreed with him. It wouldn't be very pleasant feeling uneasy every time one was alone in one's own home at night.

'Personally,' said Patsy Scott, 'I've always believed there are no ghosts in the Rectory that a good central-heating system wouldn't get rid of.'

We laughed at that, but Eleanor said, 'You can't just dismiss it like that. The Cobworths heard and felt things even if they didn't actually see anything. And so did the Bucklands before them. And you won't find anyone more level-headed than Kate Cobworth.'

Patsy shrugged. 'The Loys didn't even hear or feel anything. They'd heard the stories, they *expected* to hear the footsteps and the carriage wheels. Diana Loy told me. And Diana was quite a nervy, highly strung sort of person. But absolutely nothing happened while they were there.'

'Well, maybe the Church of England or whoever's responsible will install central heating for this new person,' I said, 'and we'll see if your theory's right, Patsy.'

Eleanor and I went home after that. We went on foot because our house is only about a quarter of a mile up Shawley Lane. On the way we stopped in front of the Rectory, which is about a hundred yards along. We stood and looked over the gate.

I may as well describe the Rectory to you before I get on with this story. The date of it is around 1760 and it's built of pale dun-coloured brick with plain classical windows and a front door in the middle with a pediment over it. It's a big house with three reception rooms, six bedrooms, two kitchens and two staircases – and one poky little bathroom made by having converted a linen closet. The house is a bit stark to look at, a bit forbidding; it seems to stare straight back at you, but the trees round it are pretty enough and so are the stables on the left-hand side with a clock in their gable and a weathervane on top. Tom Cobworth, the last rector, kept his old Morris in there. The garden is huge, a wilderness that no one could keep tidy these days – eight acres of it including the glebe.

It was years since I had been inside the Rectory. I remember wondering if the interior was as shabby and in need of paint as the outside. The windows had that black, blank, hazy look of windows at which no curtains hang and which no one has cleaned for months or even years.

'Who exactly does it *belong* to?' said Eleanor.

'Lazarus College, Oxford,' I said. 'Tom was a Fellow of Lazarus.'

'And what about this new man?'

'I don't know,' I said. 'I think all that system of livings has changed but I'm pretty vague about it.'

I'm not a churchgoer, not religious at all really. Perhaps that was why I hadn't got to know the Cobworths all that well. I used to feel a bit uneasy in Tom's company, I used to have the feeling he might suddenly round on me and demand to know why he never saw me in church. Eleanor had no such inhibitions with Kate. They were friends, close friends, and Eleanor missed her after Tom died suddenly of a heart attack and she had had to leave the Rectory. She had gone back to her people up north, taking her fifteen-year-old daughter Louise with her.

Kate is a practical down-to-earth Yorkshirewoman. She had been a nurse – a ward sister, I believe – before her marriage. When Tom got the living of Shawley she several times met Mrs Buckland, the wife of the retiring incumbent, and from her learned to expect what Mrs Buckland called 'manifestations'.

'I couldn't believe she was actually saying it,' Kate had said to Eleanor. 'I thought I was dreaming and then I thought she was mad. I mean really psychotic, mentally ill. Ghosts! I ask you – people believing things like that in this day and age. And then we moved in and I heard them too.'

The crunch of carriage wheels on the gravel drive when there was no carriage or any kind of vehicle to be seen. Doors closing softly when no doors had been left open. Footsteps crossing the landing and going downstairs, crossing the hall, then the front door opening softly and closing softly.

'But how could you bear it?' Eleanor said. 'Weren't you afraid? Weren't you terrified?'

'We got used to it. We had to, you see. It wasn't as if we could sell the house and buy another. Besides, I love Shawley – I loved it from the first moment I set foot in the village. After the harshness of the north, Dorset is so gentle and mild and pretty. The doors closing and the footsteps and the wheels on the drive – they didn't do us any harm. And we had each other, we weren't alone. You can get used to anything – to ghosts as much as to damp and woodworm and dry rot. There's all that in the Rectory too and I found it much more trying!'

The Bucklands, apparently, had got used to it too. Thirty years he had been rector of the parish, thirty years they had lived there with the wheels and the footsteps, and had brought up their son and daughter there. No harm had come to them; they slept soundly, and their grown-up children used to joke about their haunted house.

'Nobody ever seems to see anything,' I said to Eleanor as we walked home. 'And no one ever comes up with a story, a sort of background to all this walking about and banging and crunching. Is there supposed to be a murder there or some sort of violent death?'

She said she didn't know, Kate had never said. The sound of the wheels, the closing of the doors, always took place at about nine in the evening, followed by the footsteps and the opening and closing of the front door. After that there was silence, and it hadn't happened every evening by any means. The only other thing was that Kate had never cared to use the big drawing room in the evenings. She and Tom and Louise had always stayed in the dining room or the morning room.

They did use the drawing room in the daytime – it was just that in the evenings the room felt strange to her, chilly even in summer and indefinably hostile. Once she had had to go in there at ten-thirty. She needed her reading glasses which she had left in the drawing room during the afternoon. She ran into the room and ran out again. She hadn't looked about her, just rushed in, keeping her eyes fixed on the eyeglass case on the mantelpiece. The icy hostility in that room had really frightened her, and that had been the only time she had felt dislike and fear of Shawley Rectory.

Of course one doesn't have to find explanations for an icy hostility. It's much more easily understood as being the product of tension and fear than aural phenomena are. I didn't have much faith in Kate's feelings about the drawing room. I thought with a kind of admiration of Jack and Diana Loy, that elderly couple who had rented the Rectory for a year after Kate's departure, had been primed with stories of hauntings by Kate, yet had neither heard nor felt a thing. As far as I know, they had used that drawing room constantly. Often, when I had passed the gate in their time, I had seen lights in the drawing-room windows, at nine, at ten-thirty and even at midnight.

The Loys had been gone three months. When Lazarus had first offered the Rectory for rent, the idea had been that Shawley should do without a clergyman of its own. I think this must have been the

Church economizing – nothing to do certainly with ghosts. The services at St Mary's were to be undertaken by the vicar of the next parish, Mr Hartley. Whether he found this too much for him in conjunction with the duties of his own parish or whether the powers-that-be in affairs Anglican had second thoughts, I can't say; but on the departure of the Loys it was decided there should be an incumbent to replace Tom.

The first hint of this we had from local gossip; next the facts appeared in our monthly news sheet, the *Shawley Post*. Couched in its customary parish magazine journalese it said, 'Shawley residents all extend a hearty welcome to their new rector, the Reverend Stephen Galton, whose coming to the parish with his charming wife will fill a long-felt need.'

'He's very young,' said Eleanor a few days after our discussion of haunting with the Scotts. 'Under thirty.'

'That won't bother me,' I said. 'I don't intend to be preached at by him. Anyway, why not? Out of the mouths of babes and sucklings,' I said, 'hast Thou ordained strength.'

'Hark at the devil quoting scripture,' said Eleanor. 'They say his wife's only twenty-three.'

I thought she must have met them, she knew so much. But no.

'It's just what's being said. Patsy got it from Judy Lawrence. Judy said they're moving in next month and her mother's coming with them.'

'Who, Judy's?' I said.

'Don't be silly,' said my wife. 'Mrs Galton's mother, the rector's mother-in-law. She's coming to live with them.'

Move in they did. And out again two days later.

The first we knew that something had gone very wrong for

the Galtons was when I was out for my usual evening walk with our Irish Setter Liam. We were coming back past the cottage that belongs to Charlie Lawrence (who is by way of being Shawley's squire) and which he keeps for the occupation of his gardener when he is lucky enough to have a gardener. At that time, last June, he hadn't had a gardener for at least six months, and the cottage should have been empty. As I approached, however, I saw a woman's face, young, fair, very pretty, at one of the upstairs windows.

I rounded the hedge and Liam began an insane barking, for just inside the cottage gate, on the drive, peering in under the hood of an aged Wolseley, was a tall young man wearing a tweed sports jacket over one of those black-top things the clergy wear, and a clerical collar.

'Good evening,' I said. 'Shut up, Liam, will you?'

'Good evening,' he said in a quiet, abstracted sort of way.

I told Eleanor. She couldn't account for the Galtons occupying Charlie Lawrence's gardener's cottage instead of Shawley Rectory, their proper abode. But Patsy Scott could. She came round on the following morning with a punnet of strawberries for us. The Scotts grow the best strawberries for miles around.

'They've been driven out by the ghosts,' she said. 'Can you credit it? A clergyman of the Church of England! An educated man! They were in that place not forty-eight hours before they were screaming to Charlie Lawrence to find them somewhere else to go.'

I asked her if she was sure it wasn't just the damp and the dry rot.

'Look, you know me. *I* don't believe the Rectory's haunted or anywhere can be haunted, come to that. I'm telling you what Mrs Galton told me. She came to us on Thursday morning and said did I think there was anyone in Shawley had a house or a cottage to rent because they couldn't stick the Rectory another night. I asked her what was wrong. And she said she knew it sounded crazy – it did too, she was right there – she knew it sounded mad, but they'd been terrified out of their lives by what they'd heard and seen since they moved in.'

'Seen?' I said. 'She actually claims to have seen something?'

'She said her mother did. She said her mother saw something in the drawing room the first evening they were there. They'd already heard the carriage wheels and the doors closing and the footsteps and all that. The second evening no one dared go in the drawing room. They heard all the sounds again and Mrs Grainger – that's the mother – heard voices in the drawing room, and it was then that they decided they couldn't stand it, they'd have to get out.'

'I don't believe it!' I said. 'I don't believe any of it. The woman's a psychopath, she's playing some sort of ghastly joke.'

'Just as Kate was and the Bucklands,' said Eleanor quietly.

Patsy ignored her and turned to me. 'I feel just like you. It's awful, but what can you do? These stories grow and they sort of infect people and the more suggestible the people are, the worse the infection. Charlie and Judy are furious, they don't want it getting in the paper that Shawley Rectory is haunted. Think of all the people we shall get coming in cars on Sundays and gawping over the gates. But they had to let them have the cottage in common humanity. Mrs Grainger was hysterical and poor little Mrs Galton wasn't much better. Who told them to expect all those horrors? That's what I'd like to know.'

'What does Gordon say?' I said.

'He's keeping an open mind, but he says he'd like to spend an evening there.'

In spite of the Lawrences' fury, the haunting of Shawley Rectory did get quite a lot of publicity. There was a sensational story about it in one of the popular Sundays and then Stephen Galton's mother-in-law went on television. Western TV interviewed her on a local news programme. I hadn't ever seen Mrs Grainger in the flesh and her youthful appearance rather surprised me. She looked no more than thirty-five, though she must be into her forties.

The interviewer asked her if she had ever heard any stories of ghosts at Shawley Rectory before she went there and she said she hadn't. Did she believe in ghosts? Now she did. What had happened, asked the interviewer, after they had moved in?

It had started at nine o'clock, she said, at nine on their first evening. She and her daughter were sitting in the bigger of the two kitchens, having a cup of coffee. They had been moving in all day, unpacking, putting things away. They heard two doors close upstairs, then footsteps coming down the main staircase. She had thought it was her son-in-law, except that it couldn't have been because as the footsteps died away he came in through the door from the back kitchen. They couldn't understand what it had been, but they weren't frightened. Not then.

'We were planning on going to bed early,' said Mrs Grainger. She was very articulate, very much at ease in front of the cameras. 'Just about half-past ten I had to go into the big room they call the drawing room. The removal men had put some of our boxes in there and my radio was in one of them. I wanted to listen to my radio in bed. I opened the drawing-room door and put my hand to the light switch. I didn't put the light on. The moon was quite bright that night and it was shining into the room.

'There were people, two figures, I don't know what to call them, between the windows. One of them, the girl, was lying huddled on the floor. The other figure, an older woman, was bending over her. She stood up when I opened the door and looked at me. I knew I wasn't seeing real people, I don't know how but I knew that. I remember I couldn't move my hand to switch the light on. I was frozen, just staring at that pale tragic face while it stared back at me. I did manage at last to back out and close the door, and I got back to my daughter and my son-in-law in the kitchen and I – well, I collapsed. It was the most terrifying experience of my life.'

Yet you stayed a night and a day and another night in the Rectory? said the interviewer. Yes, well, her daughter and her son-in-law had persuaded her it had been some sort of hallucination, the consequence of being overtired. Not that she had ever really believed that. The night had been quiet and so had the next day until nine in the evening, when they were all this time in the morning room and they heard a car drive up to the front door. They had all heard it, wheels crunching on the gravel, the sound of the engine, the brakes going on. Then had followed the closing of the doors upstairs and the footsteps, the opening and closing of the front door.

Yes, they had been very frightened, or she and her daughter had. Her son-in-law had made a thorough search of the whole house but found nothing, seen or heard no one. At ten-thirty they had all gone into the hall and listened outside the drawing-room door and she and her daughter had heard voices from inside the room, women's voices. Stephen had wanted to go in, but they had stopped him, they had been so frightened.

Now the interesting thing was that there had been something in the *Sunday Express* account about the Rectory being haunted by the ghosts of two women. The story quoted someone it described as a 'local antiquarian', a man named Joseph Lamb, whom I had heard of but never met. Lamb told the *Express* there was an old tradition that the ghosts were of a mother and daughter and that the mother had killed the daughter in the drawing room.

'I never heard any of that before,' I said to Gordon Scott, 'and I'm sure Kate Cobworth hadn't. Who is this Joseph Lamb?'

'He's a nice chap,' said Gordon. 'And he's supposed to know more of local history than anyone else around. I'll ask him over and you can come and meet him if you like.'

Joseph Lamb lives in a rather fine Jacobean house in a hamlet – you could hardly call it a village – about a mile to the north of Shawley. I had often admired it without knowing who lived there. The Scotts asked him and his wife to dinner shortly after Mrs Grainger's appearance on television, and after dinner we got him on to the subject of the hauntings. Lamb wasn't at all unwilling to enlighten us. He's a man of about sixty and he said he first heard the story of the two women from his nurse when he was a little boy. Not a very suitable subject with which to regale a seven-year-old, he said.

'These two are supposed to have lived at the Rectory at one time,' he said. 'The story is that the mother had a lover or a man friend or whatever, and the daughter took him away from her. When the daughter confessed it, the mother killed her in a jealous rage.'

It was Eleanor who objected to this. 'But surely if they lived in the Rectory they must have been the wife and daughter of a rector. I don't really see how in those circumstances the mother could have had a lover or the daughter could steal him away.'

'No, it doesn't much sound like what we've come to think of as the domestic life of the English country parson, does it?' said Lamb. 'And the strange thing is, although my nanny used to swear by the story and I heard it later from someone who worked at the Rectory, I haven't been able to find any trace of these women in the Rectory's history. It's not hard to research, you see, because only the rectors of Shawley had ever lived there until the Loys rented it, and the rectors' names are all up on that plaque in the church from 1380 onwards. There was another house on the site before this present one, of course, and parts of the older building are incorporated in the newer.

'My nanny used to say that the elder lady hadn't got a husband, he had presumably died. She was supposed to be forty years old and the girl nineteen. Well, I tracked back through the families of the various rectors and I found a good many cases where the rectors had predeceased their wives. But none of them fitted my nanny's story. They were either too old – one was much too young – or their daughters were too old or they had no daughters.'

'It's a pity Mrs Grainger didn't tell us what kind of clothes her ghosts were wearing,' said Patsy with sarcasm. 'You could have pinpointed the date then, couldn't you?'

'You mean that if the lady had had a steeple hat on she'd be medieval or around 1850 if she was wearing a crinoline?'

'Something like that,' said Patsy.

At this point Gordon repeated his wish to spend an evening in the Rectory. 'I think I'll write to the Master of Lazarus and ask permission,' he said.

Very soon after we heard that the Rectory was to be sold. Noticeboards appeared by the front gate and at the corner where the glebe abutted Shawley Lane, announcing that the house would go up for auction on October 30th. Patsy, who always seems to know everything, told us that a reserve price of £60,000 had been put on it.

'Not as much as I'd have expected,' she said. 'It must be the ghosts keeping the price down.'

'Whoever buys it will have to spend another ten thousand on it,' said Eleanor.

'And central heating will be a priority.'

Whatever was keeping the price down – ghosts, cold, or dry rot – there were plenty of people anxious to view the house and land with, I supposed, an idea of buying it. I could hardly be at work in my garden or out with Liam without a car stopping and the driver asking me the way to the Rectory. Gordon and Patsy got quite irritated about what they described as 'crowds milling about' in the lane and trippers everywhere, waving orders to view.

The estate agents handling the sale were a firm called Curlew, Pond and Co. Gordon didn't bother with the Master of Lazarus but managed to get the key from Graham Curlew, whom he knew quite well, and permission to spend an evening in the Rectory. Curlew didn't like the idea of anyone staying the night, but Gordon didn't want to do that anyway; no one had ever heard or seen anything after ten-thirty. He asked me if I'd go with him. Patsy wouldn't – she thought it was all too adolescent and stupid.

'Of course I will,' I said. 'As long as you'll agree to our taking some sort of heating arrangement with us and brandy in case of need.'

By then it was the beginning of October and the evenings were turning cool. The day on which we decided to have our vigil happened also to be the one on which Stephen Galton and his wife moved out of Charlie Lawrence's cottage and left Shawley for good. According to the *Shawley Post*, he had got a living in Manchester. Mrs Grainger had gone back to her own home in London, from where she had written an article about the Rectory for *Psychic News*.

Patsy shrieked with laughter to see the two of us setting forth with our oil stove, a dozen candles, two torches and half a bottle of Courvoisier. She did well to laugh, her amusement wasn't misplaced. We crossed the lane and opened the Rectory gate and went up the gravel drive on which those spirit wheels had so often been heard to crunch. It was seven o'clock in the evening and still light. The day had been fine and the sky was red with the aftermath of a spectacular sunset.

I unlocked the front door and in we went.

The first thing I did was put a match to one of the candles, because it wasn't at all light inside. We walked down the passage to the kitchens, I carrying the candle and Gordon shining one of the torches across the walls. The place was a mess. I suppose it hadn't had anything done to it, not even a cleaning, since the Loys moved out. It smelled damp and there was even fungus growing in patches on the kitchen walls. And it was extremely cold. There was a kind of deathly chill in the air, far more of a chill than one would have expected on a warm day in October. That kitchen had the feel you get when you open the door of a refrigerator that hasn't been kept too clean and is in need of defrosting.

We put our stuff down on a kitchen table someone had left behind and made our way up the back stairs. All the bedroom doors were open and we closed them. The upstairs had a neglected, dreary feel but it was less cold. We went down the main staircase, a rather fine curving affair with elegant banisters and carved newel posts, and entered the drawing room. It was empty, palely lit by the evening light from two windows. On the mantelpiece was a glass jar with greenish water in it, a half-burnt candle in a saucer and a screwed-up paper table napkin. We had decided not to remain in this room but to open the door and look in at ten-thirty; so accordingly we returned to the kitchen, fetched out candles and torches and brandy, and settled down in the morning room, which was at the front of the house, on the other side of the front door.

Curlew had told Gordon there were a couple of deckchairs in this room. We found them resting against the wall and we put them up. We lit our oil stove and a second candle, and we set one candle on the windowsill and one on the floor between us. It was still and silent and cold. The dark closed in fairly rapidly, the red fading from the sky, which became a deep blue, then indigo.

We sat and talked. It was about the haunting that we talked, collating the various pieces of evidence, assessing the times this or that was supposed to happen and making sure we both knew the sequence in which things happened. We were both wearing watches and I remember that we constantly checked the time. At half-past eight we again opened the drawing-room door and looked inside. The moon had come up and was shining through the windows as it had shone for Mrs Grainger.

Gordon went upstairs with a torch and checked that all the doors remained closed and then we both looked into the other large downstairs room, the dining room, I suppose. Here a fanlight in one of the windows was open. That accounted for some of the feeling of cold and damp, Gordon said. The window must have been opened by some prospective buyer, viewing the place. We closed it and went back into the morning room to wait.

The silence was absolute. We didn't talk any more. We waited, watching the candles and the glow of the stove, which had taken some of the chill from the air. Outside it was pitch dark. The hands of our watches slowly approached nine.

At three minutes to nine we heard the noise.

Not wheels or doors closing or a tread on the stairs but a faint, dainty, pattering sound. It was very faint, it was very distant, it was on the ground floor. It was as if made by something less than human, lighter than that, tiptoeing. I had never thought about this moment beyond telling myself that if anything did happen, if there was a manifestation, it would be enormously interesting. It had never occurred to me even once that I should be so dreadfully, so hideously, afraid.

I didn't look at Gordon, I couldn't. I couldn't move either. The pattering feet were less faint now, were coming closer. I felt myself go white, the blood all drawn in from the surface of my skin, as I was gripped by that awful primitive terror that has nothing to do with reason or with knowing what you believe in and what you don't.

Gordon got to his feet and stood there looking at the door. And then I couldn't stand it any more. I jumped up and threw open the door, holding the candle aloft – and looked into a pair of brilliant golden-green eyes, staring steadily back at me about a foot from the ground.

'My God,' said Gordon. 'My God, it's Lawrence's cat. It must have got in through the window.'

He bent down and picked up the cat, a soft, stout, marmalade-coloured creature. I felt sick at the anticlimax. The time was exactly nine o'clock. With the cat draped over his arm, Gordon went back into the morning room and I followed him. We didn't sit down. We stood waiting for the wheels and the closing of the doors.

Nothing happened.

I have no business to keep you in suspense any longer for the fact is that after the business with the cat nothing happened at all. At nine-fifteen we sat down in our deckchairs. The cat lay on the floor beside the oil stove and went to sleep. Twice we heard a car pass along Shawley Lane, a remotely distant sound, but we heard nothing else.

'Feel like a spot of brandy?' said Gordon.

'Why not?' I said.

So we each had a nip of brandy and at ten we had another look in the drawing room. By then we were both feeling bored and quite sure that since nothing had happened at nine nothing would happen at ten-thirty either. Of course we stayed till ten-thirty and for half an hour after that, and then we decamped. We put the cat over the wall into Lawrence's grounds and went back to Gordon's house, where Patsy awaited us, smiling cynically.

I had had quite enough of the Rectory but that wasn't true of Gordon. He said it was well known that the phenomena didn't take place every night; we had simply struck an off-night and he was going back on his own. He did too, half a dozen times between then and the 30th, even going so far as to have (rather unethically) a key cut from the one Curlew had lent him. Patsy would never go with him, though he tried hard to persuade her.

But in all those visits he never saw or heard anything. And the effect on him was to make him as great a sceptic as Patsy.

'I've a good mind to make an offer for the Rectory myself,' he said. 'It's a fine house and I've got quite attached to it.'

'You're not serious,' I said.

'I'm perfectly serious. I'll go to the auction with a view for buying it if I can get Patsy to agree.'

But Patsy preferred her own house and, very reluctantly, Gordon had to give up the idea. The Rectory was sold for £62,000 to an American woman, a friend of Judy Lawrence. About a month after the sale the builders moved in. Eleanor used to get progress reports from Patsy, how they had rewired and treated the whole place for woodworm and painted and relaid floors. The central-heating engineers came too, much to Patsy's satisfaction.

We met Carol Marcus, the Rectory's new owner, when we were asked round to the Hall for drinks one Sunday morning. She was staying there with the Lawrences until such time as the improvements and decorations to the Rectory were complete. We were introduced by Judy to a very pretty, well-dressed woman in young middle age. I asked her when she expected to move in. April, she hoped, as soon as the builders had finished the two extra bath-rooms. She had heard rumours that the Rectory was supposed to be haunted and these had amused her very much. A haunted house in the English countryside! It was too good to be true.

'It's all nonsense, you know,' said Gordon, who had joined us.

'It's all purely imaginary.' And he went on to tell her of his own experiences in the house during October – or his non-experiences, I should say.

'Well, for goodness' sake, I didn't *believe* it!' she said, and she laughed and went on to say how much she loved the house and wanted to make it a real home for her children to come to. She had three, she said, all in their teens, two boys away at school and a girl a bit older.

That was the only time I ever talked to her and I remember thinking she would be a welcome addition to the neighbourhood. A nice woman. Serene is the word that best described her. There was a man friend of hers there too. I didn't catch his surname but she called him Guy. He was staying at one of the locals, to be near her presumably.

'I should think those two would get married, wouldn't you?' said Eleanor on the way home. 'Judy told me she's waiting to get her divorce.'

Later that day I took Liam for a walk along Shawley Lane and when I came to the Rectory I found the gate open. So I walked up the gravel drive and looked through the drawing-room window at the new woodblock floor and ivory-painted walls and radiators. The place was swiftly being transformed. It was no longer sinister or grim. I walked round the back and peered in at the splendidly fitted kitchens, one a laundry now, and wondered what on earth had made sensible women like Mrs Buckland and Kate spread such vulgar tales, and the Galtons panic. What had come over them? I could only imagine that they felt a need to direct attention to themselves which they perhaps could do in no other way.

I whistled for Liam and strolled down to the gate and looked back at the Rectory. It stared back at me. Is it hindsight that makes me say this or did I really feel it then? I think I did feel it, that the house stared at me with a kind of steady insolence.

Carol Marcus moved in three weeks ago, on a sunny day in the middle of April. Two nights later, just before eleven, there came a sustained ringing at Gordon's door as if someone were leaning on the bell. Gordon went to the door. Carol Marcus stood outside, absolutely calm but deathly white.

She said to him, 'May I use your phone, please? Mine isn't in yet and I have to call the police. I just shot my daughter.'

She took a step forward and crumpled in a heap on the threshold.

Gordon picked her up and carried her into the house and Patsy gave her brandy, and then he went across the road to the Rectory. There were lights on all over the house; the front door was open and light was streaming out on to the drive and the little Citroën Diane that was parked there.

He walked into the house. The drawing-room door was open and he walked in there and saw a young girl lying on the carpet between the windows. She was dead. There was blood from a bullet wound on the front of the dress, and on a low round table lay the small automatic that Carol Marcus had used.

In the meantime Patsy had been the unwilling listener to a confession. Carol Marcus told her that the girl, who was nineteen, had unexpectedly driven down from London, arriving at the Rectory at nine o'clock. She had had a drink and something to eat and then she had something to tell her mother, that was why she had come down. While in London she was seeing a lot of the man called Guy and now they found that they were in love with each other.

She knew it would hurt her mother, but she wanted to tell her at once, she wanted to be honest about it.

Carol Marcus told Patsy she felt nothing, no shock, no hatred or resentment, no jealousy. It was as if she were impelled by some external force to do what she did – take the gun she always kept with her from a drawer in the writing desk and kill her daughter.

At this point Gordon came back and they phoned the police. Within a quarter of an hour the police were at the house. They arrested Carol Marcus and took her away and now she is on remand, awaiting trial on a charge of murder.

So what is the explanation of all this? Or does there, in fact, have to be an explanation? Eleanor and I were so shocked by what had happened, and awed too, that for a while we were somehow wary of talking about it even to each other. Then Eleanor said, 'It's as if all this time the coming event cast its shadow before it.'

I nodded, yet it didn't seem quite that to me. It was more that the Rectory was waiting for the right people to come along, the people who would *fit* its still un-played scenario, the woman of forty, the daughter of nineteen, the lover. And only to those who approximated these characters could it show shadows and whispers of the drama; the closer the approximation, the clearer the sounds and signs.

The Loys were old and childless, so they saw nothing. Nor did Gordon and I – we were of the wrong sex. But the Bucklands, who had a daughter, heard and felt things, and so did Kate, though she was too old for the tragic leading role and her adolescent girl too young for victim. The Galtons had been nearly right – had Mrs Grainger once hoped the young rector would marry her before he showed his preference for her daughter? – but the women had been a few years too senior for the parts. Even so, they had come closer to participation than those before them.

All this is very fanciful and I haven't mentioned a word of it to Gordon and Patsy. They wouldn't listen if I did. They persist in seeing the events of three weeks ago as no more than a sordid murder, a crime of jealousy committed by someone whose mind was disturbed.

But I haven't been able to keep from asking myself what would have happened if Gordon had bought the Rectory when he talked of doing so. Patsy will be forty this year. I don't think I've mentioned that she has a daughter by her first marriage who is away at the university and going on nineteen now, a girl that they say is extravagantly fond of Gordon.

He is talking once more of buying, since Carol Marcus, whatever may become of her, will hardly keep the place now. The play is played out, but need that mean there will never be a repeat performance ...?

A Drop Too Much

Sou won't believe this, but last Monday I tried to kill my wife. Yes, my wife, Hedda. And what a loss that would have been to English letters! Am I sure I want to tell you about it? Well, you're not likely to tell her, are you? You don't know her. Besides, she wouldn't believe you. She thinks I'm the self-appointed president of her fan club.

The fact is, I'm heartily glad the attempt failed. I don't think I've got the stamina to stand up to a murder enquiry. I'd get flurried and confess the whole thing. (Yes, thanks, I will have a drink. My back's killing me – I think I've slipped a disc.)

Hedda and I have been married for fifteen years, and I can't complain she hasn't kept me in the lap of luxury. Of course, I've paid my own price for that. To a sensitive man like myself, it is a little humiliating to be known as Hedda Hardy's husband. And I don't really care for her books. It's one thing for a man to write stuff about soldiers of fortune and revolutions in South

American republics and jet-set baccarat games and seductions on millionaires' yachts, but you expect something a little more – well, delicate and sensitive from a woman. Awareness, you know, the psychological approach. I've often thought of what Jane Austen said about the way she wrote, on a little piece of ivory six inches wide. With Hedda it's more a matter of bashing away at a bloody great rock face with a chisel.

Still, she's made a fortune out of it. And I will say for her, she's generous. Not a settlement or a trust fund though, more's the pity. And the property's all in her name. There's our place in Kensington – Hedda bought that just before house prices went sky-high – and the cottage in Minorca, and now we've got this farmhouse in Sussex. You didn't know about that? Well, that's crucial to the whole thing. That's where I made my abortive murder attempt.

Hedda decided to buy it about six months ago. Funnily enough, it was the same week she took Lindsay on as her secretary. Of course she's had secretaries before, must have had half a dozen, and they've all worshipped the ground she trod on. To put it fancifully, they helped fill my cup of humiliation. (And while on the subject of cups, old man, you may re-fill my glass. Thank you.)

I'll tell you what I mean. They were all bitten by the bug of this Women's Lib rubbish, so you can imagine they were falling about with glee to find a couple like us. And though I manage to be rather vague about my financial position with most of our friends, you can't keep things like that dark from the girl who types the letters to your accountant, can you? The fact is, Hedda's annual income tax amounts to – let me see – yes, almost six times my annual income.

They were mistresses of the snide comment. What did you say?

All right, I don't mind admitting it, a couple of them were my mistresses too. I had to prove myself a man in some respects, didn't I? But Lindsay ... Lindsay's different. For one thing, she'd actually heard of me.

When Hedda introduced us, Lindsay didn't come out with that It-must-be-wonderful-to-be-married-to-such-a-famous-writer bit. She said, 'You write that super column for *Lady of Leisure*, don't you? I always read it. I'm crazy about gardening.'

My heart warmed to her at once, old man. And when Hedda'd finished making the poor sweet type about twenty replies to her awful fan letters, we went out into the garden together. She's really very knowledgeable. Imagine, she was living with her parents in some ghastly suburban hole and doing their whole garden single-handed. Mind you, though, it's living in the suburbs that's kept her so sweet and unspoiled.

Not that it was just that – I mean the gardening bit – that started our *rapport*. Lindsay is just about the most beautiful girl I ever saw. I adore those tall delicate blondes that look as if a puff of wind would blow them away. Hedda, of course, is handsome after a fashion. I daresay anyone would get a battered look churning out stuff about rapes and massacres year after year between breakfast and lunch.

The long and the short of it is that by the end of a week I was head over heels in love with Lindsay. And she feels the same about me. A virgin too, old man. What did you say? You should be so lucky? I reckon I deserved every bit of luck I could get in those utterly bloody weeks while Hedda was buying the farmhouse.

Honestly, Hedda treats me the way some men treat their wives. Pours out all her troubles, and if I don't grovel at her feet telling her how wonderful she is she says I don't know what it is to have responsibilities and that, anyway, I can't be expected to understand business. And all this because the house agent didn't phone her at the precise time he'd promised and the vendor got a bit bolshie about the price. I don't blame him, the way Hedda drives a bargain.

(Another Scotch? Oh, well, if you twist my arm.) Hedda got possession of the place in March and she had an army of decorators in and this firm to do the carpets and that one to do the furnishings. Needless to say, I wasn't consulted except about the furniture for what she calls my 'den'. Really, she ought to remember it isn't lap dogs who live in dens.

It's an extraordinary thing how mean rich people can be. And quixotic. Thousands she spent on that wallpaper and Wilton, but when it came to the garden she decided I could see to all that on my own, if you please. Hedda really has no idea. Just because I happen to know the difference between a calceolaria and a cotoneaster and am able (expertly, if I may for once blow my own trumpet) to instruct stockbrokers' wives in rose-pruning, she thinks I enjoy nothing better than digging up half an acre of more or less solid chalk. However, when I said I'd need to hire a cultivator and get God knows how much top soil and turves, she was quite amenable for her and said she'd pay.

'I don't suppose it'll come to more than a hundred or so, will it?' she said. 'With the Stock Market the way it is, I don't want to sell any more shares.' Just as if she was some poor little housewife having to draw it out of the Post Office. And I knew for a fact — Lindsay had told me — she was getting fifty thousand for her latest film rights.

She'd had the old stables at the end of the garden converted into a double garage. You can't park on the road itself, there's too much through-traffic, but there's a drive that leads down to the garage between the garden and a field. Not another house for miles, by the way. But the garden was a bloody wilderness and at that time you had to plough through brambles and really noxious-looking giant weeds to get from the garage to the house. Taking care, I may add, not to fall down the well on the way. Oh, yes, there's a well. Or there was.

'I suppose that'll have to be filled in?' I said. 'Naturally,' said Hedda. 'Or are you under the impression I'm the sort of lady who'd want to drop a coin down it and make a wish?'

I was going to retort that she'd never dropped a coin in her life without knowing she'd get a damn sight more than a wish for it, but she'd just bought me a new car so I held my tongue.

I decided the best thing would be to fill the well up with hard-core, concrete the top and make a gravel path over it from the garage entrance to the back kitchen door. It wasn't going to be a complicated job – just arduous – as the brick surround of the well lay about two inches below the level of the rest of the garden. The well itself was very deep, about forty feet, as I know from measuring with a plumb line.

However, I postponed work on the well for the time being. Hedda had gone off to the States on a lecture tour, leaving mountains of work for poor little Lindsay, a typescript to prepare about a million words long and God knows how many dreary letters to write to publishers and agents and all those people for whom the world is expected to stop when Hedda Hardy is out of the country.

Still, since Hedda had now established her base in Sussex and had all her paraphernalia there, Lindsay was down there too and we had quite a little honeymoon. I can't begin to tell you what a marvel that girl is. What a wife she'll make! – for some other lucky guy. I can only say that my wish is her command. And I don't even have to express my wish. A hint or a glance even is enough, and there's the drink I've just been beginning to get wistful about, or a lovely hot bath running or a delicious snack on a tray placed right there on my lap. It makes a change for me, old man, the society of a really womanly old-fashioned woman. D'you know, one afternoon while I happened to be taking a little nap, she went all the way into Kingsmarkham – that's our neighbouring burg – to collect my car from being serviced. I didn't have to ask, just said something about being a bit weary. And when I woke up, there was my vehicle tucked away in the garage, and Lindsay in a ravishing new dress tiptoeing about getting our tea so as not to disturb me ...

But I mustn't get sidetracked like this. Inevitably, we began to talk of the future. Women, I've noticed, always do. A man is content to take the goods the gods provide and hope the consequences won't be too bloody. It's really quite off-putting the way women, when one has been to bed with them once or twice, always say:

'What are we going to do about it?'

Mind you, in Lindsay's case I felt differently. There's no doubt, marriage or not, she's the girl for me. I'm not used to a sweet naivety in the female sex – I thought it had died with the suffrage – and to hear the assumptions Lindsay made about my rights and my earning power et cetera really did something for my ego. To hear her talk – until I put her right – you'd have thought I was the breadwinner and Hedda the minion. Well, you know what I mean. Unfortunate way of putting it.

We were bedding out plants one afternoon – yes, I said 'plants', there's no need to be coarse – when Lindsay started discussing divorce.

'You'd divide your property, wouldn't you?' she said. 'I mean, split it down the middle. Or, if you didn't think that quite fair on her, she could keep this place and that sweet cottage in wherever it is, and we could have the Kensington house.'

'Fair on her?' I said. 'My dear girl, I adore you, but you don't know you're born, do you? All these hereditaments or messuages or whatever the lawyers call them are *hers*. Hers, lovey, in *her* name.'

'Oh, I know that, darling,' she said. (By the way, she really has the most gorgeous speaking voice. I can't wait for you to meet her.) 'I know that. But when you read about divorce cases in the papers, the parties always have to divide the property. The judge makes a – a whatsit.'

'An order,' I said. 'But in those cases the money was earned by the husband. Haven't you ever heard of the Married Women's Property Act?'

'Sort of,' she said. 'What is it?'

'I'll tell you what it means,' I said. 'It means that what's mine is hers and what's hers is her own. Or, to enlarge, if she fails to pay her Income Tax I'm liable, but if I fail to pay mine nobody can get a bean out of her. And don't make me laugh, sweetheart,' I said, warming to my theme, 'but any idea you may have about division of property – well, that's a farce. There's nothing in English law to make her maintain me. If we got divorced I'd be left with the clothes I stand up in and the pittance I get from *Lady of Leisure*.'

'Then what are we going to do about it?' she said.

What a question! But, to do her justice, she didn't make any silly suggestions as to our living together in a furnished room. And she was even sweeter to me than before.

Of course, she loves me so she doesn't feel it a hardship to run around laying out my clean clothes and emptying my ashtrays and fetching the car round to the front door for me when it's raining. But I know she thought I'd have a go at Hedda, ask her to let me go and make a settlement on me. I could picture Hedda's face! Having a deeply rooted idea that she's the most dynamic and sexy thing since Helen of Troy, my wife has never suspected any of my philanderings and she hasn't an inkling of what's in the wind with Lindsay. The funny thing is, I had an idea that if I did tell her she'd just roar with laughter and then say something cutting about church mice and beggars who can't be choosers. Hedda's got a very nasty tongue. It's been sharpened up by writing all that snappy dialogue, I suppose.

Anyway when she got back she wasn't interested in me or Lindsay or all those petunias and antirrhinums we'd planted. The first thing she wanted to know was why I hadn't filled in the well.

'All in good time,' I said. 'It's a matter of priorities. The well can get filled in any time, but the only month to plant annuals is May.'

'I want the well filled in now,' said my wife. 'I'm sick of that bloody great heap of hardcore out there. If I wanted to look at rocks I'd have bought a house in the Alps.'

What I'd said about priorities wasn't strictly true. (Thanks, I will have that topped up, if you don't mind.) I didn't want to fill the well in because I'd already started wondering if there was any possible way I could push Hedda down it. It had become a murder weapon, and to fill it up with hardcore now would be like dropping one's only gun into the Thames off Westminster Bridge. Hedda hadn't made a will, but so what? As her widower, I'd get the lot. All through those hot weeks of summer while I stalled about the well, I kept thinking of Lindsay in a bikini on Hedda's private beach in Minorca – only it'd be my private beach – Lindsay entertaining guests in the drawing room in Kensington, Lindsay looking sweet among the herbaceous borders at the farm, *my* farm. And never a harsh word from her or a snide crack. I'd never again be made to feel that somehow I'd got an invisible apron on. Or be expected to – well, accede to distasteful demands when I'd got a headache or was feeling tired.

But how do you push an able-bodied woman of thirty-eight, five feet ten, 152 pounds, down a well? Hedda's an inch taller than I am and very powerful. Bound to be, I suppose, the T-bone steaks she eats. Besides, she never goes into the garden except to walk across it from the garage to the back kitchen door when she's put her Lincoln Continental away. I thought vaguely of getting her drunk and walking her out there in the dark. But Hedda doesn't drink much and she can hold her liquor like a man.

So the upshot of all this thinking was – nothing. And at the beginning of this month Lindsay went off for her three weeks' holiday to her sister in Brighton. I'd no hope to give her. Not that she'd a suspicion of what was going on in my mind. I wouldn't have involved a sweet little innocent like her in what was, frankly, a sordid business. As we kissed goodbye, she said:

'Now, remember, darling, you're to be extra specially loving to Hedda and get her to settle a lump sum on you. Then afterwards, when it's all signed, sealed and settled, you can ask for a divorce.'

I couldn't help smiling, though I felt nearer to tears. When you come across ingenuousness like that, it revives your faith in human nature. And when you come to think of it, old man, what an angel! There she was, prepared to endure agonies of jealousy thinking of me making love to Hedda, and all for my sake. I felt pretty low after she'd gone, stuck at the farm with Hedda moaning about not knowing how to get through all her work without a secretary.

However, a couple of days bashing away at the typewriter with two fingers decided her. She couldn't get a temp typist down in Sussex, so she'd go back to Kensington and get a girl at vast expense from the nearest agency. I wasn't allowed to go with her.

She stuck her head out of the Lincoln's window as she was going off up the drive and pointed to the heap of hardcore.

'Faith doesn't move mountains,' she bawled. 'The age of miracles is past. So let's see some God-damned action!'

Charming. I went into the house and got myself a stiff drink. (Thanks, I don't mind if I do.) It was fair enough being alone at the farm, though painful in a way after having been alone there with Lindsay. A couple of postcards came from her – addressed to us both, for safety's sake – and then, by a bit of luck, she phoned. Of course, I was able to tell her I was going to be alone for the next three weeks, and after that she phoned every night.

Remember how marvellous the weather was last week and the week before? Not too hot, but ideal for a spot of heavy engineering in the open air. I was just resigning myself to the fact that I couldn't put off filling in the well a day longer when I got this brilliant idea.

Oddly enough, it was television that inspired me. Hedda doesn't care for watching television, though we've got two big colour sets which she says, if you please, that she bought for my benefit. I hardly think it becomes her to turn up her nose at the medium considering what a packet she's made out of getting serials on it. Be that as it may, I don't much enjoy watching it with her supercilious eye on me, but I'm not averse to a little discriminating viewing while she's away. It must have been the Friday night I saw this old Hollywood film about some sort of romantic goings-on in the jungle. Dorothy Lamour and Johnny Weissmuller, it was that old. But the point was, there was a bit of wild animal trapping in it, and the way the intrepid hunter caught this puma thing was by digging a trough right on the path the hapless beast frequented and covering it up rather cunningly with branches and leaves.

It struck me all of a heap, I don't mind telling you. The occasion called for opening a bottle of Hedda's Southern Comfort. In the morning, a wee bit the worse for wear, I spied out the land. First of all I needed a good big sheet of horticultural polythene, but we'd already got plenty of that for the cloches in which I was going to have a stab at growing melons. Next the turves. I drove over to Kingsmarkham and ordered turves and the best quality gravel. The lot was delivered on Monday.

By that time I'd got all the surrounding ground levelled and raked over, smooth as a beach after the tide's gone out. The worst part was getting rid of the hardcore. Hedda was damned right about faith not moving mountains. It took me days. I had to pick up every chunk by hand, load it on to my wheelbarrow and cart it about a hundred yards to the only place where it could be reasonably well concealed, in a sort of ditch between the greenhouse and the boundary wall. Must have been Thursday afternoon before I got it done to my satisfaction. I remember reading somewhere that the human hand is a precision instrument that some people use as a bludgeon. I wish I could use mine as bludgeons. By the time I was done, they looked like they'd been through a mincing machine.

I waited till nightfall – not that it mattered, as there wasn't an observer for miles apart from a few owls and so on – and then I spread the polythene over the mouth of the well, weighting it down not too firmly at the edges with battens. The lot was then covered with a thin layer of earth so that all you could see was smoothly raked soil, bounded by the house terrace, the really lovely borders of annuals Lindsay and I had made, and the garage at the far end.

I was pretty thankful I'd got those turves and that gravel well in advance, I can tell you, because the next day when I went to start my new car, I couldn't get a squeak out of it. Moxon's, who service it for me, had to come over from Kingsmarkham and collect it. Some vital part had packed up, I don't know what, I leave all that mechanical stuff to Hedda. But the thing was, I was stranded without a vehicle which rather interfered with my little plan to surprise Lindsay by popping down to Brighton for her last week. She, of course, was dreadfully disappointed that she wasn't going to get her surprise. 'Why don't I come back and join you, darling?' she said when she phoned that Saturday night.

And get wind of what was going on down the garden path?

'I'd much rather be with you by the sea,' I said. 'No, I'll give Moxon's a ring Monday morning. If the car's ready I'll just have to stagger in to Kingsmarkham on the 11:15 bus and collect it. It's only an hour's run to Brighton. I could be with you by lunchtime.'

'Heaven,' said Lindsay, and so it would have been if Hedda hadn't sprung a little surprise of her own on me. Luckily – with my heavenly week ahead in view – I'd laid all those turves and made a neat gravel path from the garage to the back kitchen door when, on Sunday night, Hedda phoned. She'd got all her work done, thanks to the efficiency of the temp girl, and she was coming down in the morning for a well-earned rest. By twelve noon she'd be with me.

But I didn't feel dispirited and there didn't seem any point in phoning Lindsay. After all, we were soon going to be together for ever and ever. Before I went to bed I made a final survey of the garden. The path looked perfect. No one would have dreamt it hid a forty-foot death trap going down into the bowels of the earth.

That was last Sunday night, the night the weather broke, if you remember. It was pelting down with rain in the morning, but I had to go out to establish my alibi. I caught the 10:15 bus into Kingsmarkham to be on the safe side. When Hedda says twelve noon, she means twelve noon and not a quarter past. But, by God, I was nervous, old man. I was shaking and my heart was drumming away. As soon as the Olive and Dove opened I went in and had a couple of what the doctor would have ordered if he'd been around to do an electrocardiogram. And I chatted up the barmaid to make sure she'd know me again.

At twelve sharp I beetled down to Moxon's. Couldn't have given a damn whether the car was ready or not, but if Moxon's people were talking to me face to face at noon, the police would know I couldn't have been at the farm pushing my wife down a well, wouldn't they? The funny thing was this mechanic chappie said my vehicle had been taken back to the farm already. The boss had driven it over himself, he thought, though he couldn't be sure, having only just got in. Well, that gave me a bit of a turn and I had a very nasty vision of poor old Moxon walking up to the house to find me and … However, I needn't have worried. I was just getting on the bus that took me back when I saw Moxon himself zoom by in the Land Rover with the tow rope.

It was still pouring down when I reached home. I nipped craftily round the back way and in via the garage. Hedda's Lincoln and my little Daf were there all right, the two of them snuggled up for all the world like a couple of cuddly creatures in the mating season.

Out of the garage I went on to my super new path. And it was as I had planned, a big sagging hole edged with sopping wet turf where the well mouth was. I crept up to it as if something or someone might pop out and bite me. But nothing and no one did, and when I looked down I couldn't see a thing but a bottomless pit, old boy. Never mind the rain, I thought. I'll get into my working togs, clear the well mouth of polythene and other detritus, and call the police. Here is my wife's car, officer, but where is my wife? I suspect a tragic accident. Ah, yes, I have been out all the morning in Kingsmarkham as I can prove to you without the slightest difficulty.

I was fantasizing away like this, with the rain trickling down between my raincoat collar and my sweater, when there came – my God, I'll never forget it – the most ear-splitting bellow from the house. In point of fact, from the kitchen window.

'Where the flaming hell have you been?' Only she didn't say 'flaming', you know. 'Are you out of your God-damned mind? I come here to find the place covered with your filthy fag-ends and not a duster over it for a fortnight. Where have you been?'

Hedda.

I nearly had a coronary. No, I'm not kidding. I had the first symptoms. Dizziness and pain up my left side and in my arm. I thought I'd had it. I suppose the fact is Hedda and I do have a perfect diet, the very best of protein and vitamins, and that stood me in good stead when it came to the nitty-gritty. Well, I sort of staggered up the path and into the kitchen. There she was, hands on hips, looking like one of those whatsits – Furies or Valkyries or something. (Sorry, I've had a drop too much of your excellent Scotch.)

I could have done with a short snort at that moment. I didn't even get a cup of coffee.

'One hell of a landscape gardener you are,' Hedda yelled at me. 'A couple of drops of rain and your famous path caved in. Lucky for you it happened before I got here. I might have broken my leg.'

Her leg, ha ha! Of course I saw what had happened.

The water had collected in a pool till the polythene sagged and the battens finally gave way. I would have to run into a wet spell, wouldn't I, after the heatwave we'd been having?

'You didn't put enough of that hardcore down,' said my wife in her psychopathic-bird-of-prey voice. 'Christ, you live in the lap of luxury, never do a hand's turn but for that piddling around the peonies column of yours, and you can't even fill in a God-damned well. You can get right out there this minute and start on it.'

So that's what I did, old man. All that hardcore had to be humped back by the barrow-load and tipped down the well. I worked on it all afternoon in the rain and all yesterday, and this morning I re-made the path. It's messed up my back properly, I can tell you. I felt the disc pop out while I was dropping the last hundredweight in. Still, Hedda had bought me that German hi-fi equipment I've been dreaming of for years, so I mustn't grumble. She's not a bad sort really, and I can't complain my every wish isn't catered for, provided I toe the line. (No, I'd better not have any more. I'm beginning to get double vision, thanks all the same.)

Lindsay? I expect her back on Monday and I suppose we'll just have to go on as before. The funny thing is, she hasn't phoned since last Saturday, though she doesn't know Hedda's back. I called her sister's place this morning and the sister went into a long involved story about Lindsay going off on Monday morning, full of something about a surprise for someone – but then Hedda came in and I had to ring off.

I can use your phone, old man? That's most awfully nice of you. I don't want the poor little sweet thinking I've dropped her out of my life for ever …

The Thief

The first time she stole something Polly was eight years old. She and her mother had gone in the car to have tea with her aunt, so that she could play with her cousins, James and Lizzie. It was a fine sunny day in the middle of summer. Chairs and tables were out in the garden under a big sunshade. There was a blow-up pool and the hose was on. James and Lizzie were in swimsuits and Polly put hers on. They splashed about in the water. Polly got very excited, splashed water over her mother and Auntie Pauline and took hold of Lizzie, holding her head under the water. Her mother told her to stop and then, when Polly didn't stop, she told her again.

'Stop that at once, Polly. You're spoiling the game for the others!'

Polly had stopped for a while, then begun again, splashing with both hands. Her aunt got up, said to her, 'Come into the house. I've got something I want to show you.'

So Polly got out of the water, dried herself on a towel and followed Auntie Pauline into the house. She thought she was going to get a present. Auntie Pauline had said that once before and had given her the thing she had shown her. Not this time. As soon as they were inside and the door was shut her aunt put her over her knee and smacked her hard, ten sharp blows across her bottom. Then Auntie Pauline went back into the garden.

When her aunt had gone and left her crying, Polly had hated her. She would have liked to kill her. Rubbing her eyes, she had walked slowly through the rooms. In one of them was a desk and on the desk, lying face-down, the book Auntie Pauline was reading. Polly took it. She put it in the big bag her mother had left in the hallway. It wasn't her aunt's book but one from the Public Library. If it was missing Auntie Pauline would have to pay for it ...

When it was time to go, she and her mother got into the car and while her mother was driving Polly took the book out of her bag and hid it under her jacket. She meant to destroy it.

But how? There was nowhere to burn it. She found her mother's scissors and while her parents were watching the news on TV she went up to her bedroom and cut the book into a hundred small pieces.

Polly's mother and Auntie Pauline had a lot of talks about the missing book. Polly was always there and heard what they said. Where could the book have gone? Auntie Pauline had asked everyone, Uncle Martin and Lizzie and James and the lady who came to clean. No one knew anything about it.

'You haven't seen it, have you, Polly?' her mother asked.

Polly looked her right in the eyes. 'Oh, no, Mummy, of course I haven't.'

She was a good liar. It seemed too that she was a good thief.

In the same class at school there was a girl called Abigail Robinson. She wasn't one of Polly's crowd. Polly thought Abby was the only person in the class who didn't like her. No, it wasn't a matter of not liking. Abby really disliked her. And it was more than that; not hating but despising. Abby looked at her as if she was something dirty you trod in in the street. And she never spoke to Polly if she could help it.

One day Polly said to her, 'What's wrong with me, I'd like to know?' Abby just shrugged her shoulders. 'My mother says you've got an attitude problem,' Polly said.

Her mother hadn't said this. She knew nothing about Abby Robinson and her not speaking to Polly.

'I suppose that's a lie,' said Abby. 'Another lie. You're always lying. That's why I don't want to know you.'

Abby had a watch she was very proud of. It was gold with a dark green face and gold hands. At swimming class she left it on a shelf in the changing room and when everyone else had gone into the pool Polly hung back and took Abby's watch. She put it in the pocket of her school blazer and put the blazer in her locker.

After the class Abby couldn't find her watch and there was a hunt for it. Polly didn't stay to join the hunt. It was three-thirty, time to go home. When she got home she went into the shed where her father kept his tools and smashed the watch with a hammer. Then, carrying the pieces, she went out into the street and dropped the remains of the watch down the drain.

Everyone at school was asked about the missing watch. The head teacher asked Polly along with the rest of her class. She looked into the head teacher's eyes, stared into her eyes, and put on her honest face.

'I never saw it, Mrs Wilson,' she said. 'I haven't touched it.'

And all the time she had a little cut on her hand where a piece of broken glass had scratched her.

Stealing things from people who had upset her was something Polly did quite a lot. Only she didn't call it stealing but 'taking'. Later on, when she was older, she had a boyfriend called Tom. He was a student and he hadn't much money. Music was what he loved and he loved his CD Walkman too. Polly thought he loved it much more than he loved her. She was right, he did, and after they had been together for a year he told her he wanted them to split up.

'I can't take you lying all the time,' he said. 'I never know what the truth is any more with you. You even lie about the time you left work or where you've been if you're late or who you've met. It's just easier for you to lie so you do it.'

'I don't', she said. 'I don't. Tell me just one lie I've told.'

'You said the phone didn't ring while I was out but I know it did. It must have rung three times. That's one. You said you didn't have a drink with Alex Swain last night but I know you did. John saw you. They say that even a liar must tell more truths than lies but you tell more lies than truths.'

He said he'd be moving out the next day. She took his Walkman while he was in the shower. He had left it lying in the bedroom on a chair on top of his jacket, a round blue and silver Walkman. She picked it up, ran down the stairs with it and out into the street. The place they lived in was at a crossroads with traffic lights. It was early morning and the traffic was heavy with big lorries waiting at the red light before taking the M1 up to the north. Polly was excited and breathing heavily. When the traffic light turned green, she threw the Walkman into the road, in front of a big truck. She heard the crunching cracking sound when the huge wheels went over it.

Tom knew he had left it somewhere in the room and he hunted everywhere for it. Of course he asked Polly if she had seen it. She looked him in the eye and told him she hadn't.

'I don't believe you.'

'Believe what you like,' she said. 'I haven't seen your stupid old Walkman. You must have left it somewhere.'

What could he do about it? He walked out on her the next day but not before he told her he had seen the broken blue and silver pieces in the road.

Polly wasn't alone for long. She started seeing Alex Swain and she fell in love with him. He fell in love with her too and they moved in together. Alex was different from any boyfriend she had had before. He was five years older with a house of his own and a car and a good job. Apart from that, he was a grown-up person who made rules for life and kept them. As well as being very good-looking, Alex was kind and loving and, above all, an honest man who valued truth-telling. He often said how much he hated lying, even the kind of lies people tell to get out of going somewhere they don't want to go. Even the lies they tell to avoid hurting someone's feelings. If you spoke firmly and with kindness, he said, you need not lie.

Being with him changed Polly's life. Or she thought it had changed her life. She found that Alex trusted her. He took it for granted what she said to him was the truth. He believed everything she said. And because she loved him she mostly told him the truth. It wasn't hard to be truthful with him.

He is making me a better person, she said to herself. I am young enough to change. It's lucky for me I met him while I was still young. Another thing he did for her was that he taught her not to hate people. It wasn't worth it, he said. And now she was with him no one seemed to hurt or upset her or if they did she had learned to forget it. She no longer took other people's things and broke them. If they were unkind to her or let her down in some way, she didn't hate them as she once would have done. All that was in the past. She was different.

'I've never known you so happy, Polly,' her mother said. 'Being with Alex must be doing you good.'

And her friend Louise said, 'I thought he was a bit too much of a do-gooder but I've changed my mind now I see he's making you happy.'

2

Alex saw the suitcase before Polly did. It was quite a small suitcase, orange with a black trim and a black and orange strap, surely the only one like it in the airport.

'He won't lose it,' he said. 'No one will pick that up by mistake.'

Polly laughed. 'I'd get tired of it if it was mine.'

The man with the suitcase wore a black suit and a bright yellow shirt. He was ahead of them in the queue at the check-in and there were three people between them and him. The queue moved very slowly.

'You may as well go,' said Polly. 'There's no point in you waiting. I'll be back on Friday.'

'I just thought I'd like to see you safely through the fast-track but if you're really sure. I do have things to do.'

Alex kissed her and she watched him go back the way they had come. He looked back twice, waving. The man in black and yellow had reached the check-in desk and put his orange case on the conveyor. His name in large black letters on an orange label was easy to read: *Trevor Lant*. One thing to be said for a bag that colour, thought Polly, was that you'd see it the moment it bowled out on to the belt. There wouldn't be any puzzling over which of the black ones was yours. The man in the black suit had been given his boarding pass and was off towards the gate with his small but still orange carry-on bag. Moving up the queue, Polly forgot him.

Forgot him, that is, until he was at the gate. She saw him again then, could hardly have missed him, for Trevor Lant had taken over four of the chairs in the seating area. It looked as if the flight would be full and all those waiting wanted to sit down. Lant had spread his things out to cover those chairs, the small orange carry-on bag, two newspapers, a magazine, his suit jacket, a book and a slice of cake in plastic wrap. Polly moved into the seating area just as a woman went up to Lant and asked him if he would mind moving his things so that she and her mother could sit down.

'Yes, I would mind.' Lant stared at her. 'First come, first served. You should have got here sooner if you wanted a seat.'

The woman blushed. She had lost her nerve and walked away. An old man tried it next, then a woman with a shrill voice.

'What's with you people?' said Lant. 'Didn't you hear me the first time? I'm not moving my stuff.'

'I'm afraid you'll have to, sir.' This was one of the women from behind the desk, fetched from looking at boarding passes. 'There's a lady here who can't stand for long. Now come along, I'm sure you don't want any trouble.'

'Yes, I do,' Lant said. 'I don't mind a bit of trouble. It would liven things up a bit, would trouble. I'm getting bored out of my head in this dump. Go on, move my stuff, and you'll see what trouble is.'

Polly didn't wait to hear the outcome. She moved away and stood staring out of one of the windows at the Boeing 757 which in half an hour would start taking them all to New York. Behind him voices were raised, a crowd had gathered and men in uniform had joined in. But just as she began to think that the man in the black suit would not be allowed to stay in the seating area, the flight was called and boarding began. Trevor Lant slowly picked up his newspapers, his book, his jacket, his piece of cake and his orange carry-on bag and joined the queue.

With a club class ticket, Polly thought herself safe from him. She was almost sure she had seen an economy class ticket in his hand. But a passenger may be upgraded to a higher class and it seemed this had been done for Lant. He had been given the seat beside Polly's and would be sitting next to her for the next seven hours.

At first this seemed no problem. Lant said not a word. He gave his jacket to a member of the crew, stuffed his book and papers into the pocket in front of him and put his orange bag on the floor. His seatbelt on, he lay back and closed his eyes. He looked about thirty-five. He had dark hair, very pale skin and thin lips. She remembered that his teeth were good, his eyes blue. Most people would call him attractive but he was so very rude. I hope he won't be rude to me, she thought. I hate that.

Polly turned her head to the window, thinking that she had never known a flight to take off on time. This one left only ten minutes late. She had a book with her and the crossword puzzle in the paper to do. A trolley came round and she took a glass of wine, then another. Alex didn't like her to drink too much but Alex wasn't here. She read the paper. There was a story about an escaped Komodo dragon with a photo. It was the stuff of nightmares, a giant lizard.

Lant slept on. Polly was handed a menu and one for the man next to her. Lunch came quickly after that and the rattle of her table woke Lant. He sat up with a jerk, nearly hitting the tray the stewardess was passing her.

'You might have told me lunch was coming,' he said to Polly in a sharp tone. 'You should have woken me up.'

The stewardess caught her eye and gave a little smile. It was plain she thought Polly and Lant were partners. That was how it sounded. Polly didn't return the look or reply to Lant. He said to her, 'I'm Trevor. What's your name?'

'Polly,' she said.

He made a big fuss over putting up his table, tugging at it and pushing it too far forward. She had pasta for her main course and he had chicken curry. Polly was hungry and had eaten most of hers when Lant set down his knife and fork and said, 'How's your food, Polly? Vile, isn't it?'

This time she had to say something, though she was smarting from being treated like a doormat kind of wife. 'Mine wasn't bad.'

'You tell them that and the standard will never get better. It will just go down. I don't know what's with you people. You put up with second-class everything. Have you no taste? Don't you care?'

Before she could reply, he was saying the same thing to the stewardess who came to take their plates. She was to tell the cook, if there was a cook, to repeat his very words and come back and tell him she had done so. The stewardess said she would and Polly asked her if she would bring her another glass of wine. What Lant said next took her breath away.

'It's not a good idea drinking alcohol on flights. These glasses are very big. Each one is at least four units and you're quite a small woman.'

She wanted to say she needed it, having to sit next to him but she never said things like that. She wasn't very brave. If she was rude to him she was afraid he would insult her, make some remark about her looks or her clothes and that would hurt. He was looking over her shoulder at the photo of the giant lizard.

'I was talking to you,' he said.

'I know,' she said.

'Here's your poison coming now. Make it last. You don't want to stagger off the plane when we get there.'

The stewardess began to tell him that the chief steward had apologized. They were sorry the food hadn't been to his liking. Would he accept a glass of dessert wine?

'I don't drink,' he said. 'Give it to her. She can put any amount away.'

That was too much for Polly. She told herself, you will regret it if you don't speak up now, and said, 'Are you always so rude? I don't want to talk to you. Why can't you leave me alone?'

Her hands were shaking and he could see. He laughed. 'Poor little Polly. Was Daddy horrid then?'

She felt her face grow red. It was always the way. She could never match someone else's rudeness. Her hands would shake, she would blush and come out with words a child might use. She had other ways of dealing with it but these were not possible now. His next words surprised her.

'You know what they say. If a man's rude to a woman it's because he finds her attractive.'

'Do they?' She had never heard anyone say it.

'You are, though. Very attractive. Have dinner with me tonight?'

She wouldn't dream of it. Have him call her a poor little thing and tell her to stop drinking? Well, she could try to be rude, even if she blushed and her hands shook.

'I'd rather have dinner with the Komodo dragon,' she said very loudly.

Now she had got to him. His face went red and white and set in rigid lines. She turned away with a toss of her head and looked out of the window, seeing nothing. A voice saying 'Would you like coffee?' made her turn round. She nodded, and passed the cup from her tray. He had coffee too. They sat, staring in front of them, each with a cup of coffee.

Because she was going straight to a meeting with friends as soon as they got to New York, she was wearing a pale cream trouser suit. The airline's paper napkin was across her knees. She put milk into her coffee, stirred it. His voice saying 'Watch this' turned her head. He lifted his cup and poured a stream of coffee across her knee.

It was hot and Polly screamed. The stewardess came running.

'He poured coffee over me,' she cried. 'He poured it over me on purpose. He's mad.'

The stewardess looked from one to the other. 'I'm sure he didn't mean …'

'Of course I didn't,' Lant said. 'Of course not. I'm so sorry,

Polly. I can't tell you how sorry I am. What can I do? Can I pay your cleaning bill?'

She said nothing. She was afraid that if she spoke she would start to cry. The stewardess sponged her trousers but the stain wouldn't come out. Polly thought of how she would have to meet her friends with a big brown stain from the top of her thigh to her knee. She would have no time to change. Could they give her a different seat? The chief steward said he was sorry but there were no empty seats.

She went back to sit next to Lant. Her leg smarted where the hot coffee had touched the skin. She put the airline's blanket over her knees to cover the stain. Tears were running out of her eyes. She closed them and turned her face into the back of the seat. He was sleeping, breathing heavily, and his breathing sounded to her like laughter.

You are not a child, she told herself. Stop crying, don't let him see. I hate him, a voice inside her said, I hate him. I would like to kill him. She thought of other people she had hated like this, her Auntie Pauline, a girl at school, a boyfriend who had left her. She had had revenge on them. Revenge wasn't possible with Trevor Lant. Her tears dry now, she sat there for hours, quieter, telling herself, you will never see him again after we land. Never again.

She dozed. The captain's voice, saying they were beginning their descent for New York, woke her. Lant was still asleep.

3

With ten minutes to spare before her friends were due, Polly changed her trousers for a black pair in the hotel bathroom. Next morning she tried three dry-cleaners but they all said the stain would never come out, though one said they would try. She had come to New York to go to her cousin Lizzie's wedding and she meant to have a happy day. Before leaving for the church she spoke on the phone to Alex. She had thought to tell him about Trevor Lant and what he had said. But somehow, when she was talking to him, she couldn't. If she started that she would have to tell him what she had said to Lant when he asked her to have dinner with him. He would be shocked. He hated rudeness.

'Did you have a good flight?'

'Oh, yes. Quite good.'

'No one awful sitting next to you?'

Now would be the time to tell him. Instead, she lied. He was so kind and trusting he always believed her.

'No. The seat was empty all the way to New York.'

'I hope you'll be as lucky coming back. I miss you, darling.'

'I miss you too.'

Why had she lied to Alex? An ex-boyfriend had told her she lied when there was no need. She could have told Alex a man had sat next to her and nothing more than that. But she had lied. And it was the first time for weeks.

She went to the wedding. Her Auntie Pauline was there as the bride's mother and she greeted Polly at the church door. Polly hadn't seen her very much for years. Auntie Pauline had changed a lot and looked quite old but she was still the same woman who had smacked Polly after saying she had something to show her. As

Polly walked in and took her seat she thought again about taking the book and cutting it up. She looked at the little scar on her hand where a piece of glass had cut it. When the service started she forgot Auntie Pauline and the smacking and the book for a while and asked herself how she would feel if she was the bride and Alex the bridegroom. One day, she thought, maybe one fine day we'll get married. Next day she was taken to the theatre. Then there was shopping and lunch with the friends she had met when she first got there. She didn't see Auntie Pauline again and someone told her she had gone back on Thursday morning. It was Thursday night when Polly took a taxi to the airport. She ought to buy a present to take home for Alex but he never seemed to want anything and in the end, after looking in shop windows, she left it.

Lant's case came into view before he did. She thought, it can't be, I'm seeing things. But there it was, in the economy class queue, and there he was in his black suit, a pink shirt this time and with his orange carry-on bag. She shouldn't have said what she had said to him. He wouldn't forget it. He was the kind of man who would want revenge and she knew all about revenge.

They wouldn't up him to club class this time. Surely they wouldn't. The queue he was in moved more slowly than hers. It was far longer. When she had checked in, she turned round and met his eyes. He curled his lip and made a gesture with the middle finger of his right hand.

She felt the blood rush into her face. Please let me get to the check-in fast and get away from him. When she was given her boarding pass, she sighed with relief and walked away as fast as she could.

The gate was a long way away but she would get there first. And then – would he come and sit next to her? It would be better if she didn't get there first. Let him get there first and then she could sit far away from him. You will soon be home, she told herself, and then you really will never see him again. He can't hurt you. Anyway, he will be sitting in the economy class. She went into a little bar, meaning to have a cup of coffee. When she was sitting on the bar stool she asked for a gin and tonic instead. She needed it.

If he passed by she didn't see him. But she couldn't sit there much longer. She had to go. In ten minutes the gate would close and in twenty boarding would begin. On her way to the gate she felt that at any moment he might come up behind her. Even touch her. It was like walking in a dark street at night and knowing someone was behind you. The footfalls come nearer but you mustn't run.

She looked round. The footfalls were a woman's. He was nowhere. He must be at the gate, she thought, and he was. He must have got there while she was having her drink but she hadn't seen him. She knew he must be there but still she jumped when she saw him. She sat down as far from him as she could get. Boarding began and when she joined the line he came up to her. Turning away, she pretended not to see him but he spoke to her. There was no escape.

'Remember me?' he said.

She nodded, her mouth dry.

'I think you should say you're sorry for what you said to me.'

She found a voice, a little shrill voice. 'I will not! That dragon is lovely beside you. Now go away.'

He shouted at her. 'You bitch! You stuck-up bitch!'

One of the airport staff came up to them. 'Now, sir, please. This won't do. Please keep your voice down.'

'Tell her,' Lant said. 'She's my partner. She flies club and makes me fly economy. How about that?'

Polly felt the tears come into her eyes. Her 'I'm not, I didn't,' sounded feeble. 'Let's just get on the aircraft,' she said, a sob in her voice.

And when they did, she was sent to the left and Lant to the right. He was quiet and meek now. He had got what he wanted and made the flight crew think she was his partner. She could see that in the looks they gave her. The stewardess thought she and Lant were a couple but she had made herself the boss and she had the money. What sort of woman would make her husband or lover or boyfriend travel economy while she went club? No wonder they all looked at her like that.

Still he had gone and had no reason to come down here. Early in the morning she would be in London and she would never see him again. Alex would be there to meet her. If only he were with her now! She longed to see him. If he were with her now, to hold her hand, to comfort her, to speak to Lant in the way only he could, calmly, quietly but very sternly. She did up her seatbelt, closed her eyes, pretended Lant wasn't there.

The flight took off. The aircraft came through the cloud cover into a clear blue sky. Polly had a pre-dinner drink and a small bottle of wine with her dinner. It would help her to sleep. Just before they put out the cabin lights, the stewardess came up to her and handed her a piece of paper.

'Your partner asked me to give you this,' Polly fancied her tone was cold.

'Thank you.'

Why was the woman standing there? 'Can I get you anything before we dim the lights?'

'No, thank you. I'm fine.'

The piece of paper was folded once. She was sure the stewardess had read it. Of course she had. Polly opened it. *Don't binge-drink*, it said. *You are an alcoholic and I am keeping my eye on you.*

She would have liked to kill him. If he were beside her now she would hit him. She couldn't help herself. Often she slept on flights but now she couldn't. She kept thinking of the stewardess reading that note, telling the rest of the crew. Maybe Trevor Lant talked to them about her and asked them to keep an eye on her. Maybe he talked to the people next to him, pointed her out, said she was a worry to him.

Hit him, go down there and hit him, if only she dared. She lay awake all night, turning from side to side, thinking of Auntie Pauline hitting her in the garden. And what she had done. Long ago, twenty years ago, but still fresh in her mind.

Another note came in the morning. This time she didn't look at it. She knew it would be about her drinking. She meant to stop anyway, not because of Lant but because Alex didn't like it. Now she told herself that the club class would get off first. When they landed she would be among the first ten or twelve to get off. He would be far behind.

Getting up and moving to the exit, she took care not to look to her left. She kept her eyes fixed ahead. She was the fifth person to step off the aircraft and she walked fast. Along the passages, following the signs, keeping in fifth place, joining the EU line, showing her passport and passing through. Then and only then she looked back. Lant was nowhere to be seen.

Down the ramp to the baggage hall. Take a trolley. The bags from the New York flight started coming through soon after she got there. For the first time ever her case was one of the first to roll down the belt. She took hold of it and put it on the trolley. As she began to wheel it away she saw the orange one bounce on to the belt. Lant's orange suitcase with the black trim.

Hatred for him filled her and made her heart pound. She turned round and went back, watching the orange case go round. There was a pale blue one in front of it and a black one behind. Most of the baggage was black. His was the only orange one. She stood there, waiting – for what? For him to come? The bags were coming round again. A grey one first, then a dark red one with a strap round it, then the pale blue one. Without thinking what she was doing, Polly put out her arm, grabbed the orange case by its handle and pulled it off the belt. She put it next to hers on the trolley and wheeled it away. Her heart beat heavily. She was tense with fear and joy. She had done it, she had got back at him. This was her revenge. As soon as she could she would destroy his case. It was only when she was through Customs that she thought how the orange case would be known everywhere. No one else had one like it. Alex would know it as soon as he saw it. She went into the ladies' toilet, leaving the trolley outside. With her case and Lant's inside a cubicle, the door locked, she opened the orange case. No time to see what was in it. She pulled everything out, most of it in plastic bags but dirty clothes as well. On the outward trip her own case had been half-full of presents for Lizzie and other friends. With the presents gone, there was plenty of room. She stuffed Lant's things in and shut the lid.

The orange case must stay behind. She found a piece of paper in her handbag, and wrote on it *Out of Order*. She unlocked the door, said to the woman waiting, 'Don't go in there. It's dirty. It's a mess', and fixed the notice on the door handle. Hours would pass before they found the orange case.

All his stuff would be rubbish, she thought.

Everything he had with him would be rubbish – but not to him. The loss of it would spoil his day and next day and the next. It would cost him a lot of money. It would cause him endless trouble. Good. She would destroy it all. Of course she would. She always destroyed the stuff she took.

It was a long time since she had taken anything. Years. She remembered taking Tom's Walkman. To get back at him. To have revenge because he told her she was a liar and he couldn't stand her lying. But this must be the last. Never do it again, she told herself. You are going to be like Alex, honest, truthful, a fit wife for him ...

Lant would be in the baggage hall by now. He would be watching all the other cases coming off, all but his. He would go to that lost baggage counter you went to and tell them. It would be a long time before he guessed she had taken it – if he ever did.

Why did I do it? she asked herself as she came out into the cold London air. *Why do I do it?* Then Alex was there, kissing her, taking her own case from her. She walked beside him to the car.

'You're very silent,' he said. 'Are you all right?'

'I'm fine.'

Coming home was better than going away. Polly had felt like this only since she met Alex. Before that, home was just somewhere you slept and maybe ate your breakfast. This house was Alex's. He had bought it before she knew him and furnished it with things he had chosen carefully in colours he liked. When he first brought her here she had walked round, admiring everything. The people she knew didn't live in houses like this. It was a grown-up's house, full of pretty things Alex had looked after, china and glass and books, pictures and green plants, cushions and rugs. Polly knew Alex would have put flowers in the vases to welcome her home. Tulips and daffodils were in the hall, the first thing she saw when he opened front door.

He had to leave for work almost at once. She wanted him to go so that she could open her case. Wanting Alex to go was new. She had never felt like that before but now she was longing to open her case. Alex took it upstairs into their bedroom and put it on the bed. He kissed her good-bye and said he'd be home by six. From the window she watched him get back into the car and reverse it out of the driveway.

All the way home she had looked forward to opening it. But now it was there and she was alone a strange thing happened. Opening it no longer seemed a good idea. She went up to it and put her hands on its lid. The scar on her left hand showed up more than usual. It looked red against her pale skin. Her hands rested there for a moment and then she took them away. She told herself that she wasn't exactly afraid of what she might see. It was just that there was no need to know now, at once, at this minute, what was in those plastic bags she had taken out of the orange case. Later would do. Put it off till later.

She took the case off the bed and laid it on the seat of a chair. Then she lay down on the bed, on top of the quilt. The sunshine was very bright. Should she draw the curtains? She got up and drew them. The curtains were the colour of a cornflower and now the room was full of a blue glow. She got back on the bed and turned to face the other way. In front of her eyes was the chair and on the seat was the case. Closing her eyes, she tried to sleep but the room was too light. It was hard to keep her eyes shut but when she opened them all she saw was the case. She got up again and put it on the floor where she couldn't see it.

The triumph she had felt when she first took the orange case was gone now. Already she was wishing she hadn't taken it. Tired as she was, she knew it was no use lying there. She wouldn't sleep. After a few more minutes of lying there in the soft blue light, she got up, drew back the curtains and went downstairs. She made herself a sandwich but she couldn't eat it. What she needed was a drink to help her open that case.

She poured gin into a glass, put in an ice cube and orange juice. That made her think of how Lant had called her an alcoholic. She felt better about taking his case. He had asked for it. He had asked for what she had done, talking to her like that. The gin was a good idea. Drinking it made her think she'd be able to open the case quite soon, though she still couldn't eat her sandwich. I had my revenge, she said to herself, going upstairs again, I had my revenge. I got back at him. She didn't feel excited and happy the way she had when she took Auntie Pauline's book. When she cut up the pages with mother's scissors. Or when she took Abby Robinson's watch, smashed it with her father's hammer, pushed the bits down the drain and made that scar.

Maybe she didn't feel happy because she hadn't yet destroyed what had been in his case. Breaking or burning or cutting up the things she took always seemed to take a load off her mind. That was how she got to feel better. Those plastic bags would hold only dirty clothes and maybe things he had bought. Cheap things, not worth much, but burning them or stamping on them and putting them in the rubbish would help her. She lifted up the case and put it back on the bed.

I have to get my own clothes out, she said to herself. I have to take his things out. Don't put it off any longer. Time is passing. It's already nearly three and Alex will be home again at six.

But she did put it off. It was so long since she had taken anything of someone else's, destroyed anything. Because I didn't need to, she thought. Because I met Alex and I was happy. Was that it? I didn't tell so many lies too because I was happy. She walked to the window and looked down into the street below. Someone parked a red car on the other side. A woman came along with a small brown dog on a lead. Go back, she said to herself. Go back and open that case.

Suppose there was something dreadful inside.

But what could there be? Body parts, she thought, drugs. But no, those things would have been found. Porn? Well, if that was what it was, she would burn it. The best thing would be to burn everything. But where could she burn it? No one had open fires any more except maybe in the country. There was a metal bucket outside in the shed. She could make a fire in that. But she had never in all her life made a fire. It was something people used to do, when her mother was young.

Count to ten, she said aloud, and when you get to ten open the case. She counted to ten but she didn't open it. This was mad, this was no way to go on. She put her hands on the lid of the case and saw the scar again. She shut her eyes so that she couldn't see it, held her breath, and flung the lid open.

Lant's plastic bags lay jumbled up inside. She couldn't see what was inside them. Slowly, she took them out, laid them on the bed, feeling paper inside. She knew what was in them before she looked and she began to feel sick. One after another she opened the packets. Nothing dirty, nothing horrible. The packets were full of money, fifty-pound notes in one, US dollars in the next, euros in the third, hundreds if not thousands.

She ran into the bathroom and threw up into the basin.

4

Money was the one thing she couldn't destroy. No matter how much she might want to. She couldn't. Things, yes. A book, a watch, a Walkman. That hadn't felt like stealing but like revenge, like a trick, like getting her own back.

A man her father knew had been caught stealing money from the firm he worked for. Her mother and father had been shocked, upset, and so had she when they told her. Now she was as bad as that man, she had stolen money. She could go to prison or, because it was a first offence, get a fine and a criminal record for the rest of her life.

Telling herself that she must know, there must be no more putting off, she counted the money. Five thousand pounds, a bit less than ten thousand dollars, a bit under ten thousand euros. Yet he had flown economy class. Because he got the money in New York and he already had his return ticket? Perhaps. What did it matter? The big thing, the awful thing, was that she had stolen it.

She couldn't leave it there on the bed. Time was passing and it was nearly four. At this time of year the sun had set, the light was going. She couldn't leave Lant's dirty clothes there either. Those she stuffed into one of the plastic bags, took it downstairs and put it outside into the wastebin. The afternoon felt cold now it was getting dark. A sharp wind was blowing.

Back in the bedroom, she counted the money again. Five thousand pounds doesn't take up much room. She went to the desk she called hers, though everything in this house was really Alex's, found a large brown envelope and put the money inside. The envelope could have held twice the amount. It wasn't so bad when she couldn't see the money. When it was hidden. She took her own clothes out of the case, set some aside for washing, some for dry-cleaning.

The phone rang. She jumped and caught her breath. It would be him. It would be Trevor Lant. What could she say? Very afraid, she picked up the phone, her hand shaking.

Her voice came, breathy and shrill. 'Hello?'

It was her mother. 'I said I'd phone. Give you a chance to get home and unpack. How did the wedding go?'

'It was fine.'

'You don't sound fine. Have you got a cold?'

Polly longed to tell her. She couldn't. She knew what her mother would say: tell Alex, tell the police, say what you've done and make it all right. But first she would say, Polly, how could you? What's wrong with you? 'I'm just tired,' she said, and making an effort, 'How's Dad?'

'Better, I'm glad to say. He thought you might both come over for a meal tonight. Save you cooking.'

Her mother thought she lived like they used to thirty years ago, cooking meat and two veg, making desserts. She would know how to make a fire, burn things … 'Can we make it some other night? Tomorrow?'

'Of course, darling.'

'I'll phone.'

When she had put the phone down, the house seemed very quiet. There was no noise from the street, no wind blowing, no footsteps, no traffic sounds. It was as if she had gone deaf.

The silence made her long for sound. She put out one finger and tapped the bedhead. The tiny tap made her jump again. Then she said aloud, 'What shall I do?'

Not what her mother would have told her to do. Not what Alex would have told her. Still, it was plain she couldn't keep the money. Every moment it was in this house she was stealing it. If she took it to a police station and said what she had done, they would think she was mad. They would arrest her. She imagined their faces, staring at her as they asked her to say again what she had said. You took a man's case? But why? What were you thinking of? That was stealing – did you know that? She knew she couldn't go to the police. But she must do something. Find out where Trevor Lant lived? Yes, that was it. Find out where he lived and get his money back to him.

The phone book first. If he wasn't there she would try the Internet. He might not live in London. Still, she would try her own phone book first, the one for West London. Her hand shook as she turned the pages. Lanson, Lanssens, Lant … There were four Lants listed, one in Notting Hill, one in Maida Vale, one in Bayswater and a T.H. Lant nearer to her own house than any of them. Only half a mile or so away, in Willesden. But could she be sure it was him? She could phone and when he answered, say, 'Trevor Lant?'

He would know her voice. She knew she would be much too

afraid to phone him. Could she get someone else to do it? Not Alex, not her mother or her father. A friend? Roz? Louise? They would want to know why. The address in the phone book looked like a house, not a flat. Number 34 Bristol Road, NW2. Why had she got this crazy idea that she would know it was his house when she saw it? Did she think he would have painted it orange?

Of course she couldn't go there. He would recognize her. Not if she wore a long dark coat. Not if she tied her head up in a scarf like the Muslim women wore and put on dark glasses. Was she just going there to look? To make sure the Trevor Lant whose money she had, lived there? And how would she do that?

It was only four-thirty in the afternoon but dark by now. She should go soon if she meant to be back when Alex came home. If she was going return Trevor Lant's money she should also return his clothes. Keeping them was stealing too. Outside it was icy in the bitter wind. Her hands shaking again, she took the plastic bag out of the wastebin and for the first time looked at what was inside. Two T-shirts, two pairs of underpants, two pairs of socks, the yellow shirt he had worn on the flight out and a red shirt. She wrote a note for Alex in case she wasn't home in time: *Gone to Louise's. Back soon.* He had never liked Louise. He wouldn't phone her.

Alex had the car. She could get to Bristol Road by bus and on foot. Suddenly she was aware of how tired she was. Of course she had hardly slept at all last night and she hadn't been able to sleep when she got home. A drink would help. He had called her an alcoholic and maybe he was right. Who cared? When all this was over and the money and the clothes were back with him, she'd give up drinking. Alex would like that. No more gin, though. Not at this hour, as her mother might say. She opened a bottle of red wine and poured herself a big glass.

When she had drunk half the wine she put on her long black coat, wrapped a grey and black scarf round her head and put on dark sunglasses. This get-up made her look strange but round here a great many people looked strange. Should she take the money and the clothes with her? And then what? Leave them on his doorstep? No, find some other way of returning them. She put the envelope in the drawer of her desk, the clothes inside the washing machine, and drank the rest of the wine.

She had to wait a long time for the bus. About twenty people were waiting, mostly in silence, tired people who had been at work all day. It was very cold and a few thin flakes of snow were falling. She was glad of the scarf she had wrapped round her head. A woman stared at her as if she'd never seen dark glasses before but Polly kept them on even when the bus came.

Most people inside the bus sat silent, looking gloomy, but some chattered and laughed, drank from fizzy drink bottles, ate crisps, sandwiches, chocolate. Babies cried, children climbed over people and over seats. One of the little girls was the age Polly had been when she cut up the library book. She got off a long way from Bristol Road and began to walk.

A lot of women were dressed like her, without the glasses. No one took any notice of her. Once she had turned down a side street there were no more people.

Cars were parked nose to tail all along both sides. Lights shone dimly behind coloured curtains. A long-dead Christmas tree had been thrown out on the pavement with rubbish bags. She had looked up Bristol Road in the street atlas and was sure she knew the way but it seemed a very long way. She kept thinking she would meet him coming along. Or the footsteps following her would be his. She turned round once and then again but no one was there. When she reached the corner and saw the street name, Bristol Road, she felt too afraid to go on. Her watch told her it was nearly six. Alex would be home in ten minutes.

She clenched her icy hands, wishing she had brought gloves. She forced herself to walk, to push one foot in front of the other. Bristol Road seemed darker than the streets she had come along. The street lamps had long spaces between them. There were more trees and in front gardens there were evergreens, the kind you see in graveyards, the kind that never lose their black leaves. The sunglasses she wore made the darkness darker but she was afraid to take them off. It was a long street and she had come into it at number 188. It seemed like miles to 34 but at last she was outside its gate. Or outside the gate of 32, not daring to get too close. She held on to a fence post like an old woman afraid she might fall.

No lights were on in the house. It was in deep darkness and its front garden was full of dark bushes. A little light from a street lamp shone on the windows so that they looked like black glass. Of all the houses on this side only number 34 had a brightly painted front door. It was hard to tell the exact colour but it seemed to be yellow, the yellow of food, an egg yolk or a piece of cheese.

Plainly, no one was at home. She went almost on tiptoe up to the front window and tried to look inside. It was too dark to see much, just the shapes of dull heavy chairs and tables. She looked to see if there was a name under the doorbell, but there was nothing. The phone book had said a T.H. Lant lived here, not that *he* did. It might be a Thomas or Tim Lant. She had no way of knowing.

He might not even live in London but up north somewhere or in Wales or by the sea. She would have to come back in daylight. Tomorrow was Saturday and she could come then.

What would she say to Alex? Make some excuse. You mean, tell some lie, she said to herself. But she would *have* to. Suppose Alex were in her position, he would have to lie. But he wouldn't be, she told herself as she walked back to the bus stop, feeling weak and tired. He would never do the things I do …

5

On the way home she thought, suppose I find the police waiting for me? I can explain, she thought. I can tell them he gave it to me. Or I can say I know nothing about it. And if they want to search the house? I'll say it's my money, I'll say those are Alex's clothes … Alex opened the front door to her before she got her key out.

'I phoned Louise,' he said. 'I wanted to pick you up, take you out to dinner.' He looked hurt. 'There was something I was planning to ask you.'

Polly thought, he was going to propose to me. He was going to ask me to marry him. For once, she didn't know what to say. It was too late to go out now and she was so tired she thought she could fall asleep standing up.

'You left me a note saying you'd be there.'

'I know. I meant to go.' She was so used to him trusting her, believing everything she said, that the look on his face shocked her. But she was a good liar. She had had plenty of practice. Coming up close to him, she looked him straight in the eye. 'I got on the bus, the one that goes to Louise's road. It's only two stops. But I was so tired I fell asleep and when I woke up I was in Finchley.'

He believed her. His face had cleared and he laughed, but gently. 'You should have waited for me and I'd have taken you in the car.'

'I know you would.' She had to find out. 'What were you planning to ask me?'

He smiled. 'Don't worry about it. Another time.'

'I really need a drink.'

As she said it she thought of Trevor Lant saying she drank too much. Why had she ever spoken to him? Why hadn't she just kept silent when he spoke to her? Alex brought her a glass of wine.

'Have you eaten?' he asked.

'I don't want anything. I just want to go to bed.'

Suppose he had looked inside the washing machine? Before she went to bed, while Alex was watching the news on TV, she took out Trevor Lant's clothes. She put them in a bag and put the bag in the bottom of her wardrobe.

Tired as she was, she couldn't sleep. How to get away on her own for an hour or two in the morning? Just to go back to Bristol Road, see it in daylight, maybe talk to someone next door and find out who lived there. Alex slept beside her, still and silent as he always was. He wants to marry me, she thought. We've never really talked about it but I know he does. He'll ask me sometime this weekend. I shall say yes. Of course I will. And when we're engaged I'll make a vow to tell no more lies and never, ever steal anything again. The wine I drink at my wedding will be the last I'll ever drink.

She slept badly, and woke up to find him gone. She thought, I could tell him. I could tell him now. But no, she couldn't. Tell him she had stolen a man's case? Taken money and clothes out of it, brought them here, hidden them and gone to find where he lived? And it's not the first time, she would have to say. I took my aunt's book. I took a man's Walkman and threw it under a truck. I took Abby Robinson's watch and smashed it and gave myself this scar.

And I took other things, I took them to get back at people, a handbag from Louise once because she didn't ask me to her party. I threw it over the bridge into the canal. Alex would tell me I'm mad. Perhaps I *am* mad. He wouldn't want to be married to a woman like me.

Alex came in with tea for her. He was smiling. 'Had a good night?'

'I'm fine,' she said.

He seemed to have forgotten her note and the things she had said. 'I thought we could go out this morning and buy those books I need.'

I once stole a book and cut the pages to pieces because my aunt smacked me. Look at my finger. That's the scar where I cut myself … What would he do if she said that?

'You go,' she said. 'You won't need me.'

No bus this morning. He had taken the tube and left the car behind. She could say she had taken it to go shopping. On the way back from Bristol Road she could *go* shopping, make her lies true. She felt safer inside the car. Turning the corner into Lant's street she saw his car on the driveway before she saw the house, it was such a bright colour. A bright peacock blue, the kind of blue that hurts your eyes. And the front door, in daylight, was a sharper yellow than egg yolk.

So it *was* his house. It seemed to be. He liked bright colours, orange cases, yellow door, peacock blue car. Because she was in the car she wasn't wearing the scarf, the long coat and the sunglasses. She drove round again, slowly this time, on his side of the road. And saw just inside the rear window of his car his small carry-on case. His orange carry-on case.

That told her all she needed to know. He lived there. It was his house. All she had to do now was get it all back to him, the clothes – she would wash and iron his clothes – and the money. Driving away from Bristol Road, she thought of sending it by post. The post had been bad lately. Suppose the money got lost in the post? Find another way then, of getting it back. Someone at the wheel of a passing car hooted at her. What had she done? She didn't know. Anyway, it wasn't him, it wasn't Lant. The driver who had hooted was in a black car. She drove into the Tesco car park and went in, pushing her trolley between the fruit and vegetable racks.

If only I can get the money back to him, she thought, and not be seen, I will never take anything again. No, not 'take' – 'steal'. Use the proper word, she told herself. I stole that money just as I stole Tom's Walkman and Louise's bag.

But this has cured me. I will never do it again. It was funny how when you saw something unusual like his car, you soon saw others like it. She'd never before seen a car quite the colour of his but there was one in the Tesco car park, bright peacock blue.

Driving home, she tried to think of ways to get the money back. If his car was there, he was in. If it wasn't, he was out. That might not always be so. The car might be away being serviced or lent to a friend or in a lock-up garage somewhere. She would have to watch the house until she saw him go out. Put the money into small envelopes and once he was gone, put the envelopes through the letterbox in that yellow front door. And his clothes, neatly ironed, the yellow shirt and the red one and the orange T-shirt.

Why hadn't he told the police? That puzzled her. He must guess it was Polly who had taken his case. She had been flying club class so he would know she had got off the aircraft before him. When his case couldn't be found the first person he would think of would be her. And then when they found his case in the ladies' ... They would tell him that, and he would go straight to the airport police. So why hadn't they phoned or come here? Perhaps they had. Another peacock blue car was behind her, two cars behind her, and for a moment she felt afraid. But once she was home it had gone.

The look on Alex's face when she went in scared her. He was hardly ever angry but he looked angry now. She thought, he has been to my desk and found the money. Or the police have been here. But she was wrong. It was only that his computer had crashed and he had to call for help. Smiling now, pleased to see her, he helped her in with the bags of shopping.

'You didn't tell me we're going to see your parents tonight.'

She had forgotten. 'I forgot,' she said. 'Don't you want to? I can put them off.'

'No, I'd like to go. It's just that we said we'd go and see that film. I suppose we could go first. Shall we?'

She must keep watch on Lant's house. She had meant to go back this afternoon, see if his car was gone or stay there until he came out and drove away. Then she could put the money through his letter box ... It would have to wait, that was all. Wait all through Sunday? She wasn't due at work until midday on Monday but must she wait until Monday morning?

'Did you get a paper?'

'I forgot,' she said again. 'I'll go out again.'

'No, I'll go.'

Never before had she been so glad to see him go out. To leave her on her own. Always, in the past, she had wanted him with her. She had felt lonely and lost without him. Now his going out was a relief. She ran to her desk and opened the drawer where the money was.

She called it 'her' desk because she used it but in fact it was Alex's. Almost everything in the house was Alex's, the carpets, the curtains, the tables and chairs and beds and the kitchen things. It was just as it had been when she moved in with him. She had brought only a radio with her, a lamp or two, and some china and glass. The desk she had taken over because she was the one who sometimes worked from home. As far as she knew, he never went near it.

And he had not been near it that morning. The money was just as she had left it. Why had Lant wanted it in pounds, dollars and euros? It didn't matter. She found some envelopes, ten of them, and put the money into them, five hundred pounds in each one. Alex might never go near the desk but still the money wasn't safe there. She took the ten envelopes upstairs and put them in her underwear drawer. Then she checked on Lant's clothes. They were where she had left them, at the back of her wardrobe. If she did the washing now, his with hers, Alex might see Lant's yellow shirt and the orange T-shirt when she took them out of the machine. Better wait till tomorrow ...

He was back with his paper just as she was coming downstairs. As they walked together into the living room the phone rang. Again she thought, it will be the police. Or Lant himself. Lant.

He knows. He must have seen me this morning. She picked up the phone and said, 'Hello?'

Alex was standing behind her. She said into the phone, 'Who is that?' There was silence, no heavy breathing, just silence. 'Who *is* it?' Her voice sounded strained, panicky. There was no answer and she put the phone down.

She turned to Alex. He had sat down, the paper on his knees.

'Who was that?' he said. 'Was it someone you knew?'

'I don't know who it was,' she said, her eyes meeting his. 'He didn't speak.'

'He?'

'He, she, I told you I don't know. They didn't say anything.'

That had been a mistake, a bad mistake for a good liar to make.

Alex said in his quiet gentle way, 'When my friend George was married to his first wife, they got a lot of phone calls from one of these silent callers. If he answered, there was no one there. When she answered while George was with her she would say "Who is that?" but got no answer either. Of course he didn't know what she said when he *wasn't* with her.'

'I don't understand,' Polly said, though she did.

'Oh, well,' said Alex. 'Soon after that she went off with a chap she'd been seeing.'

After they had had lunch they went to the cinema.

Polly watched the film but after it was over she couldn't have said what it was about or even who was in it. She was thinking about the money and Lant's clothes and the phone call. Above all, the phone call. She had never had a phone call like it before. It must have been Lant. He hadn't said a word, but she knew it was Lant. He might not have seen her that morning, but he had guessed it was she who had taken his case. Somehow he had found out where she lived. Not from the phone book. Only Alex's name was in the phone book. This address was on her bags while she was waiting in the check-in queues. He must have noted it down either going to New York or coming back. But no, that must have been him in the car park. That must have been him following her. So he would know her address. Why? Because he too would want revenge?

Her address, but not her phone number ... Directory Enquiries would have given him that. Dial one-one-eight, five hundred. Get the voters' list online, then give Alex's name and address. It was easy. What would Lant do next?

Why hadn't he been to the police? What was he doing? Maybe it was something to do with the money. It might not be his. He might have stolen it. If that was the case, the last people he would go to were the police. That must be the answer.

She felt a huge relief. Lant wouldn't tell the police because the money wasn't his. But she must get it back to him. Polly thought of all the films she had seen in which gangsters had money stolen from them. Money they had stolen, but which they still thought of as theirs. The first thing they did was get revenge. Lant would do what her father called taking the law into his own hands ...

She must get the money back to him. But she must do it soon. She dared not wait till Monday. That would give him all tomorrow to get his revenge.

She must do it now. Lant might come here and harm her or, worse, Alex. As they came out of the cinema Alex said, 'I didn't think much of that, did you? Not the way that woman acted. Real life isn't like that.'

'No,' she said. 'No, you're right.'

She could remember very little of it but she knew real life wasn't like that.

6

'I have to go out again,' she said.

Alex said, 'OK, I'll come with you.'

'Oh, no, I'm going to Louise's. You won't want to come. You don't like her. I borrowed a pashmina from her before I went away and I ought to take it back.'

He said, his face a blank, 'I promise not to phone her this time.'

Polly didn't know what to say. She smiled, her face stiff, remembering. It had been Louise's birthday, her twenty-fifth. Polly had sent her a birthday card but knew nothing about the party. It was Roz who had gone to the party and, thinking Polly couldn't go, had told her about it next day. Polly remembered how hurt she had been and how angry. Not to be asked, and she was Louise's best friend! Next time she was at Louise's she went into her bedroom and took the handbag. On the way home — it was before she knew Alex — she stopped on the canal bridge in the dark. Holding the bag over the side, she let it slip down into the black shiny water. She could still hear the sound of the splash and feel a drop of water from the spray. Later she found out Louise had sent her a card, inviting her, but it had got lost in the post.

'We're due at your parents at seven.' Alex kissed her. 'Don't be long.'

'I won't,' she said. His kiss seemed to burn her as if she was guilty of some crime against him.

She was. She had lied to him again. She ran upstairs, took the money out of her underwear drawer and put it into the biggest bag she had. It was only when she was outside and in the car that she realized she had forgotten Lant's clothes. They were still dirty. She would wash them tomorrow and send them back to him by post. How easy all this would be if she – and Lant – had come back from New York on a Wednesday, if today was Thursday and Alex was at work. As it was, nothing was easy. She mustn't be long. She mustn't give Alex reason to suspect her again.

Lant's bright blue car was still on his driveway, just as it had been in the morning, but the orange carry-on bag was no longer inside it. It was later now than she had been yesterday, very cold but dry and the sky clear. Far above the street lamps and the bare tree branches she could see the curve of a bright white moon. Lights were on upstairs and down in Lant's house. Behind the curtains those lights looked orange, the colour he loved. She sat in the dark car on the other side of the street and a little way up. A car was parked in front of hers and one behind hers. If he looked out of that orange window he wouldn't be able to see her.

As the engine cooled the inside of the car grew cold. She began to shake with cold, wishing she had worn a warmer coat. It was just a quarter past six. She had hoped his car would be gone, his house in darkness, and she would quickly have been able to return the money. Suppose she were to drive round a bit, just to have the heater on. She would get warm but he might go out while she was away. It would be better to *see* him go out. She shivered with the cold, rubbed her hands and her upper arms.

At twenty to seven the upstairs light in his house went out. The two downstairs lights stayed on, the one in the front room and the one she could see in his hallway, through the glass panel above the front door. She drew a deep breath, sick with waiting. Her hands were cold as ice. It seemed like hours before that front room light went out. In fact it was ten minutes. She thought, he must go now, please let him go now, or I shall be late and then what shall I say to Alex?

I could phone him. I could phone my mother. And say what? That I'm stuck in a traffic jam? I can't leave here now, not when he'll come out at any minute. His hallway light stayed on. Maybe he left it on when he went out. People did that, *she* did that, to make burglars think someone was at home. The only thief here was herself ...

The front door opened and he came out. She thought, now I know for sure it's him. I wasn't quite sure before but now I know. In the light from a street lamp and the glass panel above his front door, she saw he was wearing the same black suit with a camel coat over it. His shirt was red, his tie red and black. He didn't look her way but got into his car, started the engine and turned on the headlights. It was three minutes to seven when he drove away.

She didn't waste any time but got out of her car, walked quickly across the street and up to the front door. On the doorstep she thought, maybe someone is in and they'll come to the door when I open the letter box. Trying to be very quiet, she pushed open the flap and put the first envelope in. No one came. There was silence. The other envelopes next, one, two, three. She thought she heard a sound from inside and her hand shook again, the way it had from the cold. Maybe there was no one there. He could have a dog or a cat that made that noise. She waited, listened. Nothing. She put the rest of the envelopes through, heard the last of them fall on to the mat.

It was five past seven.

Almost at once she moved into that build-up of traffic she meant to tell Alex about. But she was late already. Every traffic light turned red as she came up to it. The line of cars went very slowly. A light that was red for the first car had turned red again by the time she got there. In horror she watched the hand of the clock move from twenty past to twenty-five past. Lurching and jumping over the speed bumps, she reached home at twenty-five to eight. The front door was open. Alex was waiting for her on the step.

He said nothing, only shook his head a little. She ran upstairs, changed into a long skirt and sweater, combed her hair, and was in the car with him three minutes later.

'I phoned your mother,' he said, his voice cold. 'I said we'd be late. I didn't know how late.'

'I can explain,' she said. 'The traffic was terrible. I was as quick as I could be.'

He didn't reply. She thought, I wonder if he phoned Louise. I can't ask. I can never ask. The worst is over, anyway. I've given Lant back his money. Tomorrow I'll wash his clothes and iron them and on Monday morning I'll send them back. I'll never go near Bristol Road again. I'll never steal anything again or lie again or drink again, not when all this is over.

As he drove Alex said, 'Someone phoned. A man. It was about half an hour after you went out. He said he was the Komodo dragon and then he put the phone down.'

She thought she would scream and put her hand over her mouth to stop herself. Alex had his eyes on the road. 'I don't much care for jokes like that,' he said. 'The Komodo dragon is great, a wonderful big lizard, not something to make you laugh or shudder.'

Polly's voice came out like a squeak. 'I don't know who it was,' she lied.

'Maybe it was a wrong number. We seem to get a lot of those lately, don't we?'

He didn't speak another word all the way to her parents' house. He frowned when her father handed her a big glass of wine almost as soon as they were inside. She thought of Lant calling her an alcoholic. Did it mean you were an alcoholic if you needed a drink as much as she did? I did drink a lot on that flight, she thought. Alex hardly drinks at all. If we're always going to be together – and we are, please, we always are – I must drink less. I'll keep to what I said and drink my last glass at my wedding.

But she gulped down the wine. That was the second time Lant had phoned but, if Alex was right, the call had been made before she gave the money back. He would leave her alone now he had his money. He'd forget her, put all this behind him.

Her mother had made a big meal for them. Leek and potato soup first, then roast lamb, then a lemon tart. Before she took the money back Polly wouldn't have been able to eat. She could now, in spite of that second phone call. Lant had only called because he wanted his money. She was hungry and her father was refilling her wineglass to the brim.

Alex was talking now about the film they'd seen, telling her parents they ought to see it. Polly could remember nothing about it. She might as well not have been there. Then her father said something which made her blush and stare.

'You seem to have had a busy day, Polly. I saw you in Willesden this morning. I hooted and waved but you were lost in a dream.'

Deny it? A man doesn't mistake someone else for his own daughter.

'I didn't see you, Dad,' she said, not daring to look at Alex.

She remembered the black car which had hooted at her. She had thought it was her bad driving. Finishing the wine in her glass she thought, I would like to drink myself drunk, to sleep, not to have to drive home with Alex.

But she had to. As they moved out on to the road, he said, 'We have to talk, Polly.'

'Do we?'

'When we get home.'

I've never loved him so much as I do now, she thought, already in a panic. I love him. I can't lose him. He was going to ask me to marry him. Will he ask me now?

At home he said to her, in a voice she had never heard before, a voice that was cold and distant, 'I suppose you'll want another drink?'

'No,' she said. 'I've had too much.'

'At least you know it and that's something. Sit down then.' He sat facing her and took both her hands in his. 'A lot of strange things have been going on. Let's talk about it.'

Feeling her hands held in his made her feel better at once. 'Talk about what?'

'Well, I believed your story about falling asleep on the bus. But I don't believe it now. You said you were shopping this morning, but your dad saw you in Willesden. And this evening. You didn't go to Louise's. Louise told me on Friday she was away for the weekend. She was just leaving when I phoned. And then there was that fool who said he was the Komodo dragon. What's going on, Polly?'

'Nothing's going on. Really and truly. It's nothing.'

He kept hold of her hands. 'Are you seeing someone else?'

'Oh, no, of course not. Of course I'm not.'

'Sure? I'd rather know now.'

'There's nothing to know. I *promise* you. I love you, Alex. There couldn't be anyone else, not ever.'

'It's just that when you went to New York to Lizzie's wedding I thought, I could go too but she won't want me. If she'd wanted me, why didn't she ask? Is she meeting some man in New York? Is he coming back with her? And then when I met you at Heathrow you were so pleased to see me, you looked so happy, I thought I must be wrong.'

'You were wrong,' she said. 'You'd been so generous, buying me a ticket in club class. I was so grateful that I didn't want to go and leave you.' She clutched at his hands, lifted them to her lips and kissed them. 'I've never known you jealous before.'

'Oh, I was. I always was. I didn't let you see, that's all.'

7

Light-hearted now, she got up early, had the washing in the machine by eight, her washing and Alex's and Lant's clothes. It's going to be a good day, she thought. The sun was shining and it was less cold. There were pink flowers on the tree in the garden next door and tulips coming out in tubs. She took a cup of tea up to Alex. He would stay in bed to drink it while she took the things out of the washing machine. Just in case he noticed Lant's clothes.

They shared the housework. He might say he would do the

ironing. So she quickly ironed Lant's yellow shirt and a green one. By the time Alex came down, Lant's clothes were packed in a plastic bag and wrapped in brown paper, ready for the post.

It was like spring outside. She walked about, touching the new buds on the trees, smelling the air. Now everything was cleared up, she thought, Alex would ask her to marry him. He would probably ask her today. When she had taken up his tea he had said something about taking her out to lunch. It was to be at a pub on the river. Or he might wait until this evening to ask her. After dark was more romantic. They could have a June wedding. Where would they go on honeymoon? Not New York, definitely not New York, though it was said to be nice in June.

She went inside and found Alex in the kitchen.

'You've been busy,' he said. 'Do you want me to iron that lot?'

'If you like.'

It felt so good having nothing else to be afraid of, to know that she could tell the truth now. I will never tell any more lies, she said to herself. I will never tell him I've been somewhere I haven't been or done something I haven't done. I will change. I will be a different person. I will be the person he thought I was before last Friday.

He had started on the ironing, had already ironed a shirt of his own. Now he pulled out from the basket an orange T-shirt. It was Lant's.

She had missed it when she was ironing his clothes. She had done all the rest and packed them but she had missed this T-shirt. Alex lifted it up, looked at it.

'Is this yours, Polly?'

'Yes, of course,' she lied.

'A strange colour for you. Did you buy it in New York?'

'Yes, I did.'

'It looks a bit big for you. Is that the fashion?'

She nodded, sick of verbal lying.

'D'you know what that colour reminds me of?' Alex laid the T-shirt down on the ironing board. 'It reminds me of that man we saw at Heathrow. Do you remember? At the check-in? He was wearing a black suit and he had an orange case. Do you remember?'

She knew her face had gone red. 'Maybe,' she said. 'I think I do.'

'You said it'd be easy to find. You couldn't miss it.'

'Did I?'

She wished he hadn't said that. It cast a cloud over the day. While they were talking the sun had gone in. The sky was grey now. It looked like rain. Alex was ironing the T-shirt, taking special care with it because it was hers. He was better at ironing than she was. When he had finished he fetched a hanger from the hallway cupboard and hung the T-shirt on it.

There,' he said. 'Now you can wear it when we go out.'

She tried to smile. 'Oh, no, it's not warm enough. It's for summer.'

Upstairs she folded it and put it inside the parcel she would send to Lant. Now, for the first time, she began to think of him as a human being. A person with feelings, needs, loves, pain. It must have been a huge shock to him when he got his orange case back without the money. When he knew he'd lost all that money. What had he done about it? Anything? Had he told the police? He must have. Polly hadn't thought about the police since that first time, when she had come home on Friday evening and had thought they might be waiting for her. Maybe they were looking for her now ...

But she had given the money back. Every pound and dollar and euro of it. And tomorrow she was going to send him his clothes back.

Washed and ironed and neatly folded. Really, she had done him a favour. No harm had been done. All the harm had been to her and she remembered the stream of hot coffee he had poured on her cream trousers. Forget his feelings, his needs, she told herself. Forget his loves and pain. It's all over.

And she was better. Thanks to being with Alex, she was doing better. She hadn't acted as she had over Auntie Pauline's library book, cutting it into pieces. She hadn't cut Lant's money to pieces. Or destroyed it as she had Tom's Walkman and Abby's watch. She hadn't dropped it over the canal bridge as she had Louise's bag. She had taken his money back and would send the clothes back. It would have been easier to destroy the money and the clothes but she hadn't. If she could have told Alex everything, all of it from Auntie Pauline's book to Lant's money, he would have seen how much better she was now than she used to be. He would also think she had lost her mind. She could never tell him.

She dressed carefully for going out in a pale blue suit. Why did men always like you in blue? She didn't know. But she was sure that when she went downstairs Alex would say, 'You look lovely.'

It was strange how strong the urge to explain to him was. Only by telling him everything could she protect herself and be truly safe. Then if the police came he would know why. He and she would be in it together. I love that word, she thought, that word 'together'. One day, when Alex and I have been together for years, then I will tell him. When we are old I will tell him. And if he finds out long before that? I must take that risk, she thought. Isn't life one risk after another?

She went downstairs. Alex, who had finished the ironing and was sitting at the table reading the paper, said, 'You look lovely.'

'Shall we go, then?'

'I want to stop off on the way home and buy things for dinner tonight. We're going to have a special dinner.'

He was very romantic. He would probably go down on one knee. She remembered something. Two days before she went to America she had mislaid one of her rings. It had turned up the next day and she had no idea why she couldn't find it before. Now she understood. Alex had 'borrowed' it to buy an engagement ring the same size.

On the way back from lunch it started to rain. A fine drizzle at first, then a downpour. Polly stayed in the car while Alex went into shops buying smoked salmon, a duck, salad and fruit. He bought champagne too and a bottle of dessert wine. He would drink very little. It was mostly for her.

She thought about sending Lant's clothes back next day. Register the package perhaps? He would go to work, surely. She could take them back just as she had taken the money. Alex began the drive home. The traffic, usually light on a Sunday, was heavy because it was raining.

'Why do you always get traffic jams when it's wet?'

'I don't know,' he said. 'No one knows. It's one of the mysteries of life.'

If she had taken Auntie Pauline's book back and told her what she'd done, her life wouldn't have changed. Everything would have been much the same. If she'd told Abby Robinson that she was the one who had stolen her watch and had offered to pay for it, what would Abby have done? Nothing much, probably. Screamed and hit her perhaps. But Abby would have calmed down and taken the money. On the other hand, if she'd not taken Tom's Walkman and thrown it under a truck, life might have been utterly changed. They'd have stayed together. They might have married. She'd never have met Alex. So did that mean what she did was sometimes a good thing? Lying and stealing had brought her to Alex …

They were turning the corner into their street now. He had lived in this house for four years before they met. He had laid the carpets and bought the furniture as if he was making it ready for her. It would be her home for years now. Perhaps they would live there always, bring up their children there. Alex turned in at the gate and she looked up. Parked outside the house was a car the same colour as Lant's, the same bright peacock blue. You didn't see that shade very often.

She looked again. What she saw made her feel sick. It *was* Lant's car and Lant was sitting in the driving seat.

8

Alex got out, took the shopping out of the boot, came round and opened the door on the passenger side for her. He always did that. She had to get out, though she would have liked the earth to open and close over her head. Alex said, 'Let's get inside before it starts raining again.'

She followed him, not looking behind her. He unlocked the front door. A hand on her shoulder made her spin round. Trevor

Lant stood there on the path. Today he was wearing a bright red jacket. He looked her straight in the eye, the way she looked at people when she lied, but he didn't speak to her. He said to Alex, 'Who the hell are you?'

'What did you say?'

'I asked who the hell you are.'

'I might ask you the same question. This is my house.'

'And the woman with you is my girlfriend.'

Again Lant put a hand on her shoulder. 'Thanks for bringing the money back, darling. That's all I came for. You've still got some of my clothes but you can bring them back when you come over tonight.'

Polly tried to speak but she couldn't. She was shaking all over. She knew she had changed colour, but she couldn't tell if she had gone red or white. Lant said, 'Who is this chap, anyway? Your ex, I suppose.'

'Go,' Alex said in a voice she had never heard before. 'Go or I'll call the police.'

Lant shrugged. 'I'd say I don't admire your taste in men, Polly, only you've got me now.' He turned away, laughing. 'You've got your dragon now. I'll see you later.'

As the rain began again, he went back down the path, let himself out of the gate and got into his car. Everything in the street was grey but for his red jacket and his bright blue car. Alex went into the house and she stumbled in after him.

Her voice, which had gone and left her dumb, came back, a poor little thin voice. 'I can explain.'

'What is there to explain?' He sounded very tired.

He went into the kitchen and began taking all the things he had bought out of the bags and putting them in the fridge. Her voice gaining strength, she said, 'I really can explain, Alex. It's not what you think.'

He left what he was doing and looked at her. It was a stranger's face, one she thought she had never seen before.

'Let me tell you what I think,' he said. 'I know who that man was. I recognized him, though I don't know his name. He was the man at Heathrow with the orange bag. I think you met on the flight. Or maybe you knew each other before and arranged to meet at the airport. Anyway, you spent your time in New York with him. You saw him on Friday night, on Saturday morning and last night. I don't know where the money comes into this or the clothes but it doesn't matter. You can go off with him now. You won't have to tell me any more lies.'

'Alex, it wasn't like that. I took his bag at Heathrow. On the way back. And I had to get it back to him …'

Her voice failed and grew hoarse. Of course he wouldn't believe her. No one would believe her. She would have to tell him the whole thing, from the start of it when she was eight.

'My aunt hit me in the garden, so I stole her book and cut up the pages and …'

'Spare me this, Polly,' he said. 'I don't know where your aunt comes into this or your stealing that man's bag. It's all lies, isn't it? I know you tell lies. I've always known it but I thought you'd begun to change. I was wrong, that's all.'

'Alex, don't. Don't talk like this. That man is nothing to me. I barely know him. It's true I went to New York with him and came back with him. I've been to his house too but it's not the way you think …'

'Was that his T-shirt I ironed?'

'Yes, it was but I can explain …'

He didn't wait to hear what she had to say. She heard him talking to someone on the phone in the next room but not what he was saying. Then he went upstairs. Somehow she had to make him see. If she were to phone Lant, tell him about her and Alex, how she loved Alex, tell him they were going to be married, surely then … But that wouldn't work. Lant had come here on purpose to make Alex think he and Polly were having an affair. That was his revenge. He had seen, and now she could see, that everything she had done after stealing his case, made it look as if they were lovers. Her trips to his house, the lies she told, his clothes that she still had, the truth she had to tell, that he and she had gone to New York together and come back on the same flight. Could he somehow have followed her when she put the money through his door and had seen Alex waiting for her on the step?

Upstairs, Alex was in their bedroom, putting things into a case. She thought of how many times she had seen this scene in a film. The person who was leaving packing a case. The one who was left watching him do it. She felt cold in the warm room and as sick as she had when she first opened Lant's case.

'I'm going to my sister's,' Alex said. 'I just phoned her.'

'Alex, are you saying you're leaving me?'

'You've left me, haven't you?'

'Of course I haven't. I told you, this is all a stupid mistake.'

'You haven't had money from this man? You haven't got some of his clothes? You don't know where he lives?'

'Yes to all that, but I can explain …'

'I know,' he said, 'that what you're going to say will be a lie. So don't say it. At least don't make a fool of yourself now. Not when we're parting.' He closed the case.

Polly took hold of him by the arm. She held on to him with both hands as if she could keep him with her by force. 'Don't say that, please don't. I can explain if you'll let me.'

'Let me go, Polly. We're better apart. We've been happy in this house but I don't want to live here any more. You'll be with him wherever it is he lives. I shall probably sell this place, but it's too early to say …'

She was crying. She hung on to him and tried to stop him going. Gently, he pulled himself away, prised her hands off him. She fell on the bed and sobbed. Alex went down the stairs and she heard the front door close.

9

How could he do this to me? she asked herself as she lay there. How could he? I explained. I explained as much as he'd let me. He wouldn't listen. At any rate, Trevor Lant had a reason for doing what he did. He wanted revenge on me because I took his money. Giving it back wasn't enough for him. He wanted revenge and I can understand that. I know all about revenge. But Alex …

He had been totally unreasonable. She had told him she could explain and she had tried to but he wouldn't listen. He had believed Lant but not her. Just because she sometimes told lies. Everyone told lies – except him. She hadn't asked him to have such high standards for her. Who was he to judge her? Who was he to break up her whole world in ten minutes?

That morning he had been going to ask her to marry him. He would have bought the ring. She got up from the bed and looked out of the window. He had taken the car. It was his car, but how did he think she was to get around? It was cruel what he had done and she hated him for it.

An idea came to her and she moved across to 'his' chest of drawers. Well, all the furniture was his, but this was the chest he kept his own things in. She opened one drawer after another. His clothes were in them, socks, ties, sweaters, all but the bottom drawer which he had emptied when he packed. She tried the bedside cabinet on his side. A book, an old wallet, a watch he never wore. He hadn't taken any of his suits and only one jacket. She went through the pockets of his raincoat, his leather jacket. All the pockets were empty except for one in his overcoat. There was a jeweller's box in there, a little square box of red velvet.

She lifted its lid. The ring was inside. It was made of gold with a single large square-cut diamond. He knew her size so it would fit. It did and she slipped it on. The light caught the diamond and made a rainbow on the wall. She would never have the right to wear it now. He would come back for the rest of his clothes when he knew she'd be at work, take the ring away and give it to some other woman. Wherever he went to live he would need his furniture, so he would take that too. All the love she had had for him turned to hate.

She would have liked to have a big van come round. The men in it would take out all his tables and chairs and glass and china and put it in the van. They would take it somewhere, it didn't matter where, and she would smash it all up. There was no van and no men. She was on her own but she could still do it.

She went downstairs and into the living room. With one movement of her arm, she swept all the ornaments off a shelf. Glass broke and china and the leg came off a wooden horse. He had broken up her world and she would break up his. It would be the biggest destruction she had ever done. She picked up the CD player and hurled it against the wall, pulled the CDs out of their sleeves and bent them in two. The TV screen was tough but it broke the second time she kicked it. The glass in the pictures cracked when she stamped on them. She pulled his books from the shelves and tore off their covers.

At first it seemed there wasn't much she could do to his furniture, but she fetched a sharp carving knife from the kitchen and slashed at the chair covers, scored grooves in the wood, stabbed at cushions and let their stuffing out. The curtains hung in ribbons when she had used the kitchen scissors on them. After that she ran about the house, the knife in her hand, slashing at everything she came upon. She pulled open the drawer of the drinks cabinet, poured vodka down her throat, smashed the necks of red wine bottles against the fridge and the oven, poured the wine over the pale carpet.

She drank from the broken bottles too, cutting her mouth. The drink got to her at last, making her wild at first, then stupid, dizzy, flat on the floor among the mess. She lay there, unconscious, her arms stretched out and the diamond on her finger winking in the dying light.

The Long Corridor of Time

On the evening of their first day, when they had hung their pictures and unpacked their wedding presents – tasks they hadn't cared to entrust to her mother or to the moving men – they went for a walk in the square. They walked along the pavement in the September twilight, admiring the pale gleaming façades of the terraces which, now divided into flats, had once been the London residences of the very rich. Then, when they had completed their little tour and had examined all four sides of the square, Marion took his hand and led him toward the wilderness of trees and shrubs which formed its centre.

It was a gloomy place where only the tall trees – a plane, a walnut and a catalpa – seemed to flourish. A few attenuated rosebushes struggled for life in the shadowy corners, their wan flowers blighted with mildew. Marion put her hand on the gate in the iron railings.

'It's locked,' she said.

'Of course it is, darling. It's a private garden for the tenants only. The head porter gave me our key just now.'

'Do let's go in and explore it.'

'If you like, but there doesn't seem much to explore.'

She hesitated, holding the key he had handed her, looking through the railings at the small patchy lawn, the stone tablet and the wooden, seat. 'No,' she said. 'Tomorrow will do. I *am* rather tired.'

He was touched, knowing how anxious she always was to please him. 'It's hardly the sort of garden you've been used to, is it?'

She smiled but said nothing.

'Do you know darling, I feel very guilty. I've taken you away from the country, from your country things – your horses, the dogs – everything. And all I've given you is this.'

'You didn't *take* me, Geoffrey. I came of my own free will.'

'Hmm. I wonder how much free will we really have. If you hadn't met me, you'd be at the university now – you'd have your own friends, young people. I'm twice your age.'

'Oh, no,' she said seriously as they walked back to the terrace where their flat was. 'I'll be eighteen next week. You were twice my age when we got engaged and I was seventeen and five months. Exactly twice. I worked it out to the day.'

He smiled. The head porter came out, holding the door open for them. 'Good night, madam. Good night, sir.'

'Good night,' said Geoffrey. So she had worked it out to the day. The earnest accuracy of this, a sort of futile playfulness, seemed to him entirely characteristic of the childhood she hadn't quite left behind. Only five or six years ago perhaps she had been writing with comparable precision, inside exercise books: *Marion Craig,*

The Mill House, Sapley, Sussex, England, Europe, The World, The Universe. And now she was his wife.

'He called me madam,' she said as they went up in the elevator. 'No one ever did that before.' With his arm round her and her head on his shoulder she said, 'You'll never be twice my age again, darling. That isn't mathematically possible.'

'I know that, my love. You've no idea,' he said, laughing, 'what a tremendous comfort that is.'

It wasn't true, of course, that he had given her nothing but a dusty scrap of London shrubbery to compensate for the loss of The Mill House. He asked himself which of her friends, those schoolgirls who had been her bridesmaids, could expect even in five years' time a husband who was a partner in a firm of stockbrokers, a five-room flat in nearly the smartest part of London, a car of her own parked in the square next to her husband's Jaguar and a painting for her drawing-room wall that was almost certainly a Sisley.

And he wouldn't stand in her way, he thought as he looked in his bedroom glass before leaving for work, scrutinizing his dark head for those first silver hairs. She could still ride, still have parties for people her own age. And he would give her everything she wanted.

He glanced down at the fair head on the pillow. She was still asleep and on her skin lay the delicate bloom of childhood, a patina that is lighter and more evanescent than dew and is gone by twenty. He kissed her tenderly on the side of her folded lips.

'It bothers me a bit,' he said to Philip Sarson who came out as he was unlocking his car. 'What is Marion going to do with herself all day? We don't know anyone here but you.'

'Oh, go shopping, go to the cinema,' said Philip airily. 'When I suggested you take the flat I thought how handy the West End would be. Besides, married women soon find their hands full.'

'If you mean kids, we don't mean to have any for years yet. She's so young. God, you do talk like a Victorian sometimes.'

'Well, it's my period. I'm steeped in it.'

Geoffrey got into his car. 'How's the new book coming?'

'Gone off to my publisher. Come round tonight and I'll read you some bits?'

'No, you come to see us,' said Geoffrey, trying to sound enthusiastic. A jolly evening for Marion, he thought, a merry end to the day for an eighteen-year-old – coffee and brandy with a tired stockbroker of thirty-five and an historian of forty-five. He would ask her first thing he got back what she thought about it and if there were the least hesitancy in her manner, he would phone Philip and put him off.

'But I'd like to see him,' she said. 'I love hearing about Victorian London. Stop worrying about me.'

'I expect I shall when we've settled in. What did you do today?'

'I went to Harrods and matched the stuff for the dining-room curtains and I arranged for my driving lessons. Oh, and I explored the garden.'

'The garden? Oh, that bit of jungle in the middle of the square.'

'Don't be so disparaging. It's a dear little garden. There are some lovely old trees and one of the porters told me they actually get squirrels in there. It's been such a hot day and it was so quiet and peaceful sitting on the seat in the shade.'

'Quiet and peaceful!' he said.

She linked her arm through his and touched his cheek with one gentle finger.

'I don't want to be a gadabout all the time, Geoffrey, and I've never been very wild. Don't you like me the way I am?'

He put his arms round her, emotion almost choking him. 'I love everything about you. I must be the luckiest man in London.'

'I know exactly what you mean,' said Philip when, two hours later, Marion resumed her praises of the garden. 'It *is* peaceful. I used to sit out there a lot last summer, working on my book, *Great-Grandfather's London*. I've passed many a happy hour in that garden.'

'Yes, but you're practically a great-grandfather yourself,' Geoffrey retorted. 'I want Marion to go out with her contemporaries.'

'Very few of her contemporaries can afford to live in Palomede Square, Geoff. But I'm glad you like it, Marion. I'm thinking of writing a book about the square itself. I've unearthed some fascinating stories and a lot of famous people have lived here.' Philip named a poet, an explorer and a statesman. 'These houses were built in 1840 and I think that 130 years of comings and goings ought to make a good read.'

'I'd like to hear some of those stories one day,' said Marion.

In her long black skirt she looked like a schoolgirl dressed up for charades. She must get out and buy clothes, Geoffrey thought, spend a lot of money. He could afford it.

Philip had begun to read from his manuscript and during the pauses, while Marion asked questions, Geoffrey thought – perhaps because they had all been mentally transported back more than 100 years – of those Victorian dresses which were once more so fashionable for the very young. He imagined Marion in one of them, a ruched and flounced gown with a high, boned collar and long puff sleeves. In his mind's eye he saw her as a reincarnation of a nineteenth-century ingenue crossing the square, her blonde hair combed high, walking with delicate tread toward the garden.

Smiling at Philip, nodding to show he was still listening, he got up to draw the curtains. But before he pulled the cords, he looked out beyond the balcony to the empty square below, with its lemony spots of lamplight and its neglected, leafy, umbrageous centre. Between the canopy of the ilex and the dusty yellow-spotted laurel he made out the shape of the stone cable and, beside it, the seat that looked as if it had never been occupied.

The corners of the garden were now deep caverns of shadow and nothing moved but a single leaf which, blown prematurely from the plane tree, scuttered across the sour green turf like some distracted insect. He pulled the curtain cords sharply, wondering why he suddenly felt, in the company of his loved wife and his old friend, so ill at ease.

'How was your driving lesson, darling?'

'It was nice,' she said, smiling up at him with a kind of gleeful pride. 'He said I was very good. When I came back I sat in the garden learning the Highway Code.'

'Why not sit on the balcony? If I'd been at home today I'd have sunbathed all afternoon on that balcony.'

She said naively, 'I do wish you could be home all day,' and then, as if feeling her way with caution, 'I like the garden best.'

'But you don't get any light there at all. It must be the gloomiest hole in London. As far as I can see, no one else uses it.'

'I'll sit on the balcony if you want me to, Geoffrey. I won't go in the garden if it upsets you.'

'*Upsets* me? What an extraordinary word to use. Of course it doesn't *upset* me. But the summer's nearly over and you might as well make the best of what's left.'

While they had been speaking, standing by the windows which were open onto the balcony, she had been holding his arm. But he felt its warm pressure relax and when he looked down at her he saw that her face now had a vague and distant look, a look that was both remote and secretive, and her gaze had travelled beyond the balcony rail to the motionless treetops below.

For the first time since their wedding he felt rejected, left out of her thoughts. He took her face in his hand and kissed her lips.

'You look so beautiful in that dress – sprigged muslin, isn't it? – like a Jane Austen girl going to her first ball. You didn't wear that for your driving lesson?'

'No, I changed when I came in. I wanted to put it on before I went into the garden. Wasn't that funny? I just had this feeling I ought to wear it for the garden.'

'I hoped,' he said, 'you were wearing it for me.'

'Oh, darling,' she said, and now he felt that she was with him once more, 'I can understand it upsets you when I go into the garden. I *quite* understand. I know it could affect some people like that. Isn't it strange that I know? But I won't go there again.'

He didn't know what she meant or why his simple distaste for the place – a reasonable dislike that was apparently shared by the other tenants – should call for understanding. But he loved her too much to bother with it, and the vague unease he felt passed when she told him she had telephoned one of her bridesmaid friends and been invited to a gathering of young people. It gratified him that she was beginning to make a life of her own, planning to attend with this friend a course of classes. He took her out to dinner, proud of her in her flounced lilac muslin, exultant at the admiring glances she drew.

But he awoke in the night to strange terrors which he couldn't at first define. She lay with one arm about his shoulders but he shook it off almost roughly and went quickly to get a glass of water as if, distressingly, mystifyingly, he must get away from her for a moment at all costs.

Sitting in the half-dark drawing room, he tried to analyze this night fear and came up with one short sentence: I am jealous. Never in his life had he been jealous before and the notion of jealousy had never touched their marriage. But now in the night, without cause, as the result of some forgotten dream perhaps, he was jealous. She was going to a party of young people, to classes with young people. Why had he never before considered that some of those contemporaries whom he encouraged her to associate with would necessarily be young men? And how could he, though rich, successful, though still young in a way, compete with a youth of twenty?

A sudden impulse came to him to draw back the curtains and look down into the garden, but he checked it and went back to bed. As he felt her, warm and loving beside him, his fears went and he slept.

'That's a very young chap teaching Marion to drive,' said Philip who worked at home all day, gossiped with the porters and knew everything that went on. 'He doesn't look any older than she.'

'Really? She didn't say.'

'Why should she? He won't seem young to her.'

Geoffrey went up the steps. He had forgotten his key.

'Is my wife in, Jim?' he said to the head porter. 'If not you'll have to open up for me.'

'Mrs Gilmour is in the garden, sir.'

'In the *garden?*'

'Yes, sir. Madam's spent every day this week in the garden. The gardener's no end pleased about it, I can tell you. He said to me only this morning, "The young lady" – no disrespect, sir, but he called her the young lady – "really appreciates my garden, more than some others I could name."'

'I don't get it,' said Geoffrey as he and Philip went down into the square. 'I really don't. She promised me she wouldn't go there again. I honestly do think she might keep the first promise she's made to me. It's a bit bloody much.'

Philip looked curiously at him. 'Promised you she wouldn't go into the garden? Why shouldn't she?'

'Because I told her not to, that's why.'

'My dear old Geoff, don't get so angry. What's come over you? I've never known you to get into such a state over a trifle.'

Through clenched teeth Geoffrey said, 'I am not accustomed to being disobeyed,' but even as he spoke, as the alien words were ground out and Philip stood still, thunderstruck, he felt the anger that had overcome him without any apparent will of his own seep away, and he laughed rather awkwardly. 'God, what a stupid thing to say! Marion!' he called. 'I'm home.'

She had been sitting on the seat, a book on the table in front of her. But she hadn't been reading it, for although it was open, the pages were fast becoming covered with fallen leaves. She turned a bemused face toward him, blank, almost hypnotized; but suddenly she seemed to regain consciousness. She picked up her book, scattered the leaves, and ran toward the gate.

'I shouldn't have gone into the garden,' she said. 'I didn't mean to but it looked so lovely and I couldn't resist. Wasn't it funny that I couldn't resist?'

He had meant to be gentle and loving, to tell her she was always free to do as she pleased. The idea that he might ever become paternalistic, let alone autocratic, horrified him. But how could she talk of being unable to resist as if there were something tempting about that drab autumnal place?

'I really don't follow you,' he said. 'It's a mystery to me.' If tempered with a laugh, if accompanied by a squeeze of her hand, his words would have been harmless. But he heard them ring coldly and – worse – he felt glad his reproof had gone home, satisfied that she looked hurt and a little cowed.

She sighed, giving the garden a backward glance in which there was something of yearning, something – was he imagining it? – of deceit. He took her arm firmly, trying to think of something that would clear the cloud from her face, but all that came out was a rather sharp, 'Don't let's hang about here. We're due at my cousin's in an hour.'

She nodded compliantly. Instead of feeling remorse, he was irritated by the very quality that had captivated him, her childlike naivety. A deep and sullen depression enclosed him, and while they were at his cousin's party he spoke roughly to her once or twice, annoyed because she sat silent and then, illogically, even more out of temper when she was stirred into a faint animation by the attentions of a boy her own age.

From that evening onward he found himself beginning to

look for faults in her. Had she always been so vague, so dreamy? Had that idleness, that forgetfulness, always been there? She had ceased to speak of the garden. All those jaded leaves had fallen. The thready plane twigs hung bare, the evergreens had dulled to blackness, and often in the mornings the stone table, the seat and the circle of grass were rimed with frost. The nights drew in at four o'clock and it was far too cold to sit in the open air.

Yet when he phoned his home from his office, as he had increasingly begun to do in the afternoons, he seldom received a reply. Nothing had come of that plan to go to classes and she said she never saw her friend. Where, then, was she when he phoned?

She couldn't be having daily driving lessons, each one lasting for hours. He might have asked her but he didn't. He brooded instead on her absences and his suppressed resentment burst into flames when there was no dinner prepared for their guests.

'They'll be here in three-quarters of an hour!' He had never shouted at her before and she put up her hand to her lips, shrinking away from him.

'Geoffrey, I don't know what happened to me but I forgot. Please forgive me. Can't we take them out?'

'People will begin to think I've married some sort of crazy child. What about last week when you "forgot" that reception, when you "forgot" to write and thank my cousin after we'd dined there?'

She had begun to cry.

'All right,' he said harshly. 'We'll take them to a restaurant. Haven't much choice, have we? For God's sake, get out of that bloody dress!'

She was again wearing the lilac muslin. Evening after evening when he got home he found her in it – the dress he had adored but which was now worn and crumpled, with a food spot at the waist.

He poured himself a stiff drink. He was shaking with anger. The arguments in her favour he had put forward when she forgot the reception – that there had been a dozen gatherings which she hadn't forgotten but had graced – now seemed invalid in the face of this neglect.

But when she came back into the room his rage went. She wore a dress he hadn't seen before, of scarlet silk, stiff and formal yet suited to her youth, with huge sleeves, a tight black and gold embroidered bodice, and long skirt. Her hair was piled high and she walked with an unfamiliar aloofness that was almost hauteur.

His rage went, to be replaced oddly and rather horribly by an emotion he hadn't supposed he would ever feel toward her – a kind of greedy lust. He started forward, slopping his drink.

'Damn, Isabella, but you're a fine woman!'

Incredulously, she stopped and stood still. '*What* did you say?'

He passed his hand across his brow. 'I said, "God, Marion, you're a lovely girl."'

'I must have misheard you, I really thought … I feel so strange, Geoffrey, not myself at all sometimes and you're not you. You do still love me?'

'Of course I love you. Kiss? That's better. My darling little Marion, don't look so sad. We'll have a nice evening and forget all about this. Right?'

She nodded but her smile was watery, and the next day when he phoned her at three there was no reply although she had told him her driving lesson was in the morning.

Philip looked very comfortable and at home in the armchair by the window, as if he had been there for hours. Perhaps he had. Was it possible that she was out with him, Geoffrey wondered, on all those occasions when he phoned and got no answer?

The dress he had come to hate was stained with mud at the hem as if she had been walking. Her shoes were damp and her hair untidy. Maybe she devoted her mornings to the 'very young chap' and her afternoons to this much older one. The husband, he had always heard, was the last to know.

She sat down beside him on the sofa, very close, almost huddled with him. Geoffrey moved slightly aside. What had happened to her gracious ways, that virginal aloofness, which had so taken him when he first saw her in her father's house? And he recalled, while Philip began on some tedious story of Palomede before the square was built, how he had ridden over to Cranstock to call on her father and she had been there with her mother in the drawing room, the grey-brown head and the smooth fair one bent over their work. At a word from her father she had risen, laying aside the embroidery frame, and played to them – oh, so sweetly! – on the harpsichord ...

He shook himself, sat upright. God, he must have been more tired than he had thought and had actually dozed off. When had she ever done embroidery or played to him anything but records? And where had he got the name Cranstock from? The Craigs lived in Sapley and her father was dead.

The brief dream had been rather unpleasant. He said sharply, 'Anyone want a drink?'

'Nothing for me,' said Philip.

'Sherry, darling,' said Marion. 'Did you say a *manor* house, Philip?'

'Remember all these inner suburbs were villages in the early part of the nineteenth century, my dear. The Hewsons were lords of the manor of Palomede until the last one sold the estate in 1838.'

His ill temper welling, Geoffrey brought their drinks. What right had that fellow to call *his* wife 'my dear,' and who cared, he thought, returning to catch Philip's words, if some Hewson had been a minor poet or another had held office in Lord Liverpool's government?

'The last one murdered his wife.'

'In that garden,' said Geoffrey rather nastily, 'and they took him up the road to Tyburn and hanged him.'

'No, he was never brought to trial, but there was a good deal of talk and he was never again received in society. He married a wife half his age and suspected her of infidelity. She wasn't quite sane – what we'd now call mentally disturbed – and she used to spend hours wandering in the manor gardens. They extended over the whole of this square, of course, and beyond. He accused her of having trysts there with her lovers. All imagination, of course – there was no foundation for it.'

Geoffrey said violently, 'How can you possibly know that? How can *you* know there was no foundation?'

'My dear Geoff! Because the young lady's diary happens to have come into my hands from a great-niece of hers.'

'I wouldn't believe a word of it!'

'Possibly not, but you haven't read it. There's no need to get so cross.'

'No, please don't, darling.'

He shook off the small hand which touched his sleeve. 'Be silent, Marion! You know nothing about such matters and shouldn't talk of them.'

Philip half rose. He said slowly, 'And you accuse *me* of being Victorian! What the hell's got into you, Geoffrey? I was simply telling Marion a tale of old Palomede and you fly into a furious temper. I think I'd better go.'

'Don't go, Philip. Geoffrey's tired, that's all.' Her lips trembled but she said in a steady voice, 'Tell us what became of Mr Hewson and his wife.'

The historian said stiffly, 'In the end he took her away to Italy where she was drowned.'

'You mean *he* drowned her?'

'That's what they said. He took her out in a boat in the Bay of Naples and he came back but she didn't. After that he was black-balled in his clubs and even his own sister wouldn't speak to him.'

'What God-awful romantic tripe,' said Geoffrey. He was watching his wife, taking in every slatternly detail of her appearance and thinking now of the City banquet he and she were to attend in the week before Christmas. All summer during their engagement he had looked forward to this banquet, perhaps the most significant public occasion of his year, and thought how this time he would have a beautiful young wife to accompany him. But was she beautiful still? Could she, changed and waiflike and vague as she had become, hold her own in the company of those mannered and sophisticated women?

He phoned her on the afternoon of that dim December day, for she had had a slight cold in the morning, had awakened coughing, and he wanted to be sure, firstly that she was well enough to go, and secondly that she would be dressed and ready on time. But the phone rang into emptiness.

Alarmed and apprehensive, he called Philip, who was out, and then the driving school to be told that Mrs Gilmour's instructor was out too. She couldn't be out with both of them and yet …

He got home by six. It was raining. A trail of wet footmarks led from the elevator to the door of their flat like the prints left by someone who has been called unexpectedly from a bath. And then, even before he saw the damp and draggled figure, still and silent in front of the balcony windows, he knew where she had been, where she had been every day.

But instead of calming his jealousy, this revelation somehow increased it and he began shouting at her, calling her a slut, a failure as a wife, and telling her he regretted their marriage.

The insults seemed to pass over her. She coughed a little. She said dully, remotely, 'You must go alone. I'm not well.'

'Of course you're not well, mooning your life away in that foul garden. All right, I'll go alone, but don't be surprised if I don't come back!'

Geoffrey drank more than he would have if she had been with him. A taxi brought him home to Palomede Square just after midnight and he went up the elevator, not drunk but not quite sober either. He opened their bedroom door and saw that the bed was empty.

There were no lights on in the flat except the hall light which he had just put on himself. She had left him. He picked up the phone to dial her mother's number and then he thought, no, she wouldn't go to her mother. She would go to that driver chap or to Philip.

Philip lived in a flat in the next house. Geoffrey came down the steps into the square and was on the pavement, striding to the next doorway, when he stopped and stared into the garden. At first he thought it was only a pale tree trunk that he could see or a bundle of something dropped behind the stone table. He approached the railings slowly and clasped his hands round the cold wet iron. It was a bundle of clothes, but the clothes enwrapped the seated and utterly still figure of his wife. He began to tremble.

She wore the lilac dress, its skirt sodden with water and clinging to the shape of her legs, and over it her mink coat, soaked and spiky like a rat's pelt. She sat with her hands spread on the table, one gloved, the other bare, her face blank, wax-white, lifted to the rain which fell steadily upon her and dropped sluggishly from the naked branches.

He opened the gate and went up to her without speaking. She recoiled from him but she didn't speak either. He dragged her from the seat and brought her out of the garden and into the house, half carrying her. In the elevator she began to cough, sagging against the wall, water dripping from her hair which hung in draggles under the slackened scarf that wrapped it, water streaming down her face.

Heat met them as he unlocked the door of the flat. Transiently, he thought as he pushed her inside, what have we come to, we who were so happy? A drunken autocrat and a half-crazed slattern. What has come over us?

The warmth of the radiator against which she leaned made steam rise from her hair and coat. What have we come to, he thought, and then all tender wistfulness vanished, spiralling away down some long corridor of time, taking with it everything that remained of himself and leaving another in possession.

The lamp in the square lit the flat faintly with a sickly yellow radiance. He put on no lights. 'I demand an explanation,' he said.

'I cannot explain. I have tried to explain it to myself but I cannot.' Beneath the coat which she had stripped off, over the soaked and filthy dress, she wore an ancient purple and black wool shawl, moth-eaten into holes.

'What is that repellent garment?'

She fingered it, plucking at the fringes. 'It is a shawl. A shawl is a perfectly proper article of dress for a lady to wear.'

Her words, her antiquated usage, brought him no astonishment. They sounded natural to his ears.

'Where did you obtain such a thing? Answer me!'

'In the market. It was pretty and I needed a shawl.'

He felt his face swell with an onrush of blood. 'To be more fitting for your low lover, I daresay? You need not explain why you absent yourself from my household, for I know why. You have assignations in that garden, do you not, with your paramours? With my young coachman and that scribbler fellow Sarson?'

'It is not true,' she whispered.

'Do you give me the lie, Isabella? Do you know that I could have a Bill of Divorcement passed in Parliament and rid myself of you? I could keep all your fortune and send you back to your papa at Cranstock.'

She came to him and fell on her knees. 'Before God, Mr Hewson, I am your honest wife. I have never betrayed you. Don't send me away, oh, don't!'

'Get up.' She was clinging to him and he pushed her away. 'You have disgraced yourself and me. You have committed the worst sin a woman can commit, you have neglected your duties and brought me into disrepute before my friends.'

She crept from him, leaving a trail of water drops on the carpet.

'I shall think now what I must do,' he said. 'I want no scandal, mind. Perhaps it will be best if I remove you from this.'

'Do not take me from my garden!'

'You are a married woman, Isabella, and have no rights. Pray remember it. What you wish does not signify. I am thinking of my reputation in society. Yes, to take you away may be best. Go now and get some rest. I will sleep in my dressing room and we will tell the servants you are ill so that there may be no gossip. Come, do as I bid you.'

She gathered up her wet coat and left the room, crying quietly. The lamp in the square had gone out. He searched for a candle to light him to bed but he could not find one.

Philip Sarson came into the porters' office to collect his morning paper. 'A bit brighter today,' he said.

'We can do with it, sir, after that rain.'

'Mrs Gilmour not out in the garden this morning?'

'They've gone away, sir. Didn't you know?'

'I haven't seen so much of them lately,' said Philip. 'Gone away for Christmas, d'you mean?'

'I couldn't say. Seven a.m., they went. I'd only just come on duty.' The head porter looked disapproving. 'Mr Gilmour said she was ill but she could walk all right. Tried to get into the garden, she did, only he'd taken the key away from her. She got hold of the gate and he pulled her off very roughlike, I thought. It's not the sort of thing you expect in this class of property.'

'Where have they gone? Do you know?'

'They took his car. Italy, I think he said. Yes, it was. I saw Naples on their luggage labels. Are you all right, sir? All of a sudden you look quite ill.'

Philip made no reply. He walked down the steps, across the square, and looked through the railings into the garden. A small white glove, sodden and flat as a wet leaf, lay on the seat. He shivered, cursing the writer's imagination that led him into such strange and improbable fancies.

In the Time of his Prosperity

The pyramid was separated from the lawn by a sheet of water, its reflection doubling it, adding a triangle to a triangle, with nothing between but a long, thin tongue of green. But while the pyramid was still as a rock, its image trembled when a breeze touched the water and dimpled the surface. Behind were trees, a dense screen of them, between the grey, step-sided stone temple and the sky.

Temple was Paul Hazlitt's word for it. Even then he called it that. It was four-sided, and each side took the form of a flight of nine deep steps. On the side facing him, the steps were bisected by a staircase, steep and composed of many treads, which led up to a stone house on the top, a mausoleum or an altar. It looked very old, as if it had stood there since ancient times, yet there was no moss on its northern aspect and no lichen on its roof.

He gazed at the reality and at its quivering silvery image, and saw what he had not at first noticed, two little islands in the lake, one with a tree growing on it, one bare and green. A small rowing boat was moored at the nearer shore. The temple's reflection shook with sudden violence as a gust of wind snatched at it. Paul exclaimed aloud. The man who was to employ him, the man on whose account he was there, said, 'If the pyramid of Tezcatlipoca impresses you, come into the house and I will show you wonders.'

All this I knew from the first, because it is recorded in Paul's diary, though to call it a diary is to aggrandize it. It was small and thin, with a space three inches by one-and-a-half allotted for each day. The account of Paul's arrival at Mandate Benedict is the longest entry, one of only three to hold more than the bare details of an appointment or a comment on the weather.

It seems to have been the first he ever kept, this black, leather-bound book for the year 1963. My father gave it to him because it was one of seven that had come in the post that Christmas. A diary for me, a diary for each of my brothers. I don't know what happened to the rest except for the one that went to Paul. I remember his effusive thanks, his disproportionate pleasure, but he was like that, ardent, enraptured by small things. He had come down from Oxford six months before and was living with us in London, looking for a job.

His grandmother died about that time. He went up north and was with her for a week before her death. She was the last close relative he had, for his parents were long dead, and we were distant enough, my father his second cousin and the rest of us, of course, removed even further. That winter he settled down with us and became part of our family.

He had an art-history degree and was supposed to be clever. I thought he was the most beautiful man I had ever seen. 'Handsome, not beautiful,' my mother said. 'A man can't be beautiful.'

But Paul was. His face had the sweetness of a girl's and the firm regularity of a man's. He was dark and his eyes were dark blue. He was tall and slender and straight-backed, but the most remarkable thing about his appearance – and I remember this clearly after what is, after all, quite a long time – was its flawlessness.

It sounds ridiculous, doesn't it? This is a man of twenty-two I am talking about. Perhaps it is tasteless to quote this now but I must. I must use those words and say that he was 'without a single corporal blemish'. Of course, I don't precisely know this, I never saw him totally naked, but I did see him in swimming trunks one day when we all went to the pool, and I watched him for a long time as, after coming out of the water, he lay on a towel in the sun. There were no scars on his body. That in itself is not unusual – there are none on mine – but Paul had no moles, either, not one.

These days he could have worked as a model, as a way of making a living before something more suited to his gifts came along. His grandmother had left him nothing. If there had been any insurance money from his parents' deaths, it was all gone by then. But in those days modelling was for girls to do, not men. And Paul seemed unaware of his looks. I never saw him glance covertly into a mirror; he took no special trouble over his appearance.

He had a beautiful speaking voice. I would have liked him to read aloud to me but I lacked the courage to ask him. Sometimes he played our Bechstein, though he always denied his ability when we praised him, and he never sat down at the piano without first being asked or asking permission. His manners were gentle. I never saw him lose his temper.

I have made him out a paragon, but this he was not, as we were all soon to realize. Even then we knew he was secretive, carefully keeping to himself what he did when out of our sight, telling us he was going out but not where he was going. He was secretive and a little sly, but he was not very subtle about it. Even then I understood that he expected people to believe whatever he told them. I suppose he was naive. Perhaps young people still were at that time, for isn't 1963 called the year when sex was discovered? He called my parents 'Uncle' and 'Auntie'. If he never actually used adjectives like 'ripping' and 'super', I once heard him say after some outing or gathering that he had had a smashing time. The diary – I had better call it that – has the entry for 10 February, 'Fantastic Sunday lunch at Auntie Joan's!' and for 8 March, 'A real job offer, can't believe my luck!' He was liberal throughout with that mark of exclamation journalists call the 'screamer'. You could hear it in his speech, too, in his enthusiasms and his fervour.

But the job, I must get back to that. He already had one, of sorts, in a gallery in Vigo Street, where he was paid a little if he sold a painting and nothing if he did not. For all that, my father said that what Declan Roche did was unethical, to go into the Peacock Gallery and pretend to buy a picture when his true purpose was to tempt away an employee. Tempt him first with an invitation to dine, for after hum-ing and ha-ing over this painting (of a jaguar hunt somewhere in Central America) and eyeing Paul openly all the while, Roche had asked him to have dinner with him that evening. Even I, and I was six years younger than Paul, would have seen through that one. But in the event I would have been wrong, for Roche appeared as innocent as Paul himself, and more open.

The offer he made was genuine and was enticing enough: For making an inventory of certain artefacts Paul would receive a real salary, as much as the curator of the Peacock was paid, and perquisites that seemed unbelievable: a flat, the use of a car. The disadvantage was that the contract was only for one year, from April to April, but as my mother said, it might well be extended if Paul 'gave satisfaction'.

That expression of hers, absurd, with a faintly lewd connotation, yet old-fashioned, stuck in my mind to surface again years later when I met Rosie Thornton. To make me ask myself, did he give satisfaction? And what kind of satisfaction might that have been?

But it was a long time before I asked those questions, before any speculations were made about Paul except the aggrieved kind: Why did he do it? What made him change? For we were offended. We were hurt. My father had given him the hospitality of his house for months, my mother had fed him, my brothers had befriended him, and as for me – I suppose I had had a powerful teenage crush on him. And he had repaid us by writing my father two short letters and by fleeing to Mexico as soon as his contract with Roche came to an end.

Instead of the phone call to tell us he was leaving, instead of the postcard, came the diary. Paul had left it behind at Mandate House and Roche had sent it on. His accompanying letter presupposed that we knew where Paul was and when he had gone, but it also made excuses for his former employee. It was only natural, Roche wrote, that Paul, after his experience at Mandate House and with a year's salary of which he had spent very little, should wish to go off and see the remains of the Aztec civilization for himself.

'He might have let us know,' my mother said.

And my father spoke those words that are some of the saddest in the language. 'We were mistaken in him.'

It seemed so unlike Paul. Had the warmth all been a sham, then? Under the gentle manners and the sweetness, for there is no other word for it, under the impetuous delight taken in quite ordinary things, the bubbling fervour and the simple joy, had there been a cynical opportunist who used us and cast us aside when our usefulness was over? That kind of thing is always hard to take, no less hard when you are middle-aged than when you are as young as I was. We want gratitude, even when we say we don't expect it.

My parents ignored the diary. Why send it to them? To keep it for a man who might come back one day or might not? In any case, they wouldn't have dreamt of reading it. They wouldn't have read anyone's diary. I was less honourable. One day I found it on my father's desk, and it was then that I came upon that longest entry, the one about the pyramid reflected in the lake and Roche promising to show Paul wonders. I was seventeen by then and I should have known better, but I succumbed to temptation. I found the letter written to my father in May and the letter written in August and I read those, too. My excuse must be that I had been in love, in the throes of first love, and rejection made me sore at heart.

The only other entries in the diary that were more than bare memoranda were devoted to descriptions of the objects in Roche's house. Some of the objects, that is, for as Paul points out at once, the collection was vast, it filled whole big rooms of this big house, priceless artefacts crowded or even tumbled together like junk in an attic. It was his task to set them in some sort of order, to catalogue them, to arrange them. In the first letter he wrote to my father he lists some of them more precisely: the fifteenth-century skull carved from rock crystal – 'like glass, like contemporary work in glass' – the figurine of the Goddess of the Jade Petticoat, the jade plaques, the carved yoke that was an accoutrement of Tez-catlipoca, God of the Smoking Mirror, the clay cups, the palmate stone of the sacrificed man. But above all he names the greatest of Roche's wonders, the Mandate Codex.

It meant nothing to me then. This was years before I married Michael and came to live here at this university and learned from my husband something about those things. I barely knew what a codex was and would very likely have defined the word as meaning 'cipher' or 'system'. I skimmed through what Paul said about it and passed on to his trivial daily entries: 'Rained all day,' 'Started to learn Nahuatl!,' 'Spanish improving,' 'Went into Exeter with D.R. and Andrew,' 'Hair quite long! As fashion decrees!,' 'Rain has come back.' In the August letter are more details of the collection, identified and specified in his catalogue. His handwriting was beautiful, too, small but not too small, shapely, mature, a fit vehicle to describe the ceramic flutes, the mantles of agave fibre, a feathered serpent in stone, a monkey vase in obsidian. And he was learning the flute, something apparently he had always wanted to do, for unfortunately there was no piano in Mandate House, and he must have music. His Spanish teacher, Rafael, was also a virtuoso on the flute. Everyone was tremendously nice to him, it was not a place in which to be lonely, he was scarcely if ever alone ...

No more letters came, not even a postcard. The nearest we got to news of Paul, and it was not very near, was a profile of Declan Roche than appeared in a Sunday newspaper. He was sixty-five then, unmarried, though he had had three wives, from the last of whom he was divorced in 1960. Paul was mentioned as the 'young art historian' who had set Roche's 'fabulous collection of Inca antiquities' — even in those days I knew they had got that wrong — in the order in which it could be seen at the present time.

Five or six years later Roche died. His obituary described him as a millionaire, a traveller in Central America, and a collector of works of Mesoamerican art that were the envy of museums worldwide. He had died of natural causes. His body was found by his butler Andrew Freeman on the lowest of the nine steep steps that formed the southern aspect of a pyramid in his garden at Mandate Benedict, South Devon. This pyramid was a copy, the writer of the obituary said, of the temple of the God of the Smoking Mirror at Tenochtitlán in the Templo Mayor Precinct in Mexico. I wished I could see a picture of it. I thought of its original as the principal wonder Paul had gone there to see. In my mind I held confused images of snakes with feathers, paintings of storm gods and fire gods, stone faces, and spotted cats, and I supposed he had gone there to see them, too.

The next thing I read about Roche was that, after bequests to his secretary, Nigel Coombs, his valet, Peter Smith, and Andrew Freeman, he had left everything he possessed to the British Museum, including the Mandate Codex. It was there, in the Mexican Room, that I saw the codex, some fifteen years after I had last seen Paul Hazlitt. And I saw it in the company of the woman who had been his girlfriend.

The Aztecs (I now know) made paper from tree bark pressed into sheets and coated with white pigment. They had no alphabet, no writing, so they set down their ceremonies, their mythology and their terrible blood rites in glyphs: small, sinister, and beautiful pictures in scarlet and gold, black and green and crimson, gods and men and priests, serpents and eagles and jaguars, flutes and torches and flowers. The most famous of these books or codices, according to Michael, is probably the Codex Florentinus in Florence. This one, which had been Roche's, had been hidden by a priest of Tezcatlipoca in, of all places, a recess behind the altar of a Christian church. An earthquake had brought it to light and its discoverer had sold it to Roche, reprehensibly, certainly illegally, for an undisclosed sum. It was a treasure. Even to those, like me, who knew nothing of the mythology, the ritual, or the history, it was exquisite.

'Strange that a people who were so cruel could make such beautiful things,' Rosie Thornton said.

'It happens,' I said, 'and not just in Mexico.'

She had asked me to meet her there. My father had had a letter from her in which she said she was in search of Paul. She had tried old college friends of his, an old school friend, his grandmother's neighbours, all in vain. My parents could be of no more help to her than those others, but she left them a phone number in case they heard of anyone who might know, in case anything came up.

Curiosity impelled me to phone her and make that appointment. Had she been his girlfriend in the particular sense in which this differs from a mere friend? Strangely enough, I don't know. Rosie Thornton never really said, only that they knew each other because Paul's grandmother and her mother were friends. They had known each other since they were children. She gave a sad smile when she said that, not at all surprised that my parents had never heard of her, taking Paul's concealment of her existence for granted. I suppose that in her way she was as noncommittal as he, though not so secretive as to keep his letters to herself. Not that there was anything in them that the whole world might not have seen, not a word of love, no reference to any intimacy. She showed them to me on the following day in her flat in Gower Street.

'I thought he'd just dropped me,' she said. 'But when my mother died and I tried to get in touch with him and couldn't, that worried me. He'd been fond of my mother and I knew he'd want to know. I tried everyone. And now I've met you, and you say he's never been in touch with any of you, I don't know what to think.'

The first letter she had from Paul seemed to have been written on the same day in August as the one to my father. It had much the same information in it, details of the flutes, the agave mantle, the monkey vase and a description of Rafael, his flute teacher, who was also teaching him Spanish and Nahuatl.

'What's Nahuatl?' I said.

'The language those people spoke. I don't know why he had to learn anything. He didn't go to Mandate to learn but to make an inventory.'

The life he led was more luxurious than anything he had previously known. Rather ingenuously, he described his private bathroom. Every evening he and Roche sat down to a four-course dinner with nine feet of mahogany table between them, Roche at the head and he at the foot. Roche's servants waited on him as if he were more honored a guest than he had any right to be.

That was in August. In his December letter he described the house and the grounds and gave a detailed picture of the Pyramid of Tezcatlipoca. Roche, he said, had had it built five years before from Dartmoor granite. He was an eccentric, self-made and an autodidact, obsessed with what he had seen on his travels in Central America, a fanatic about pre-Hispanic history, ignorant yet passionate, totally involved with Aztec and Mayan mythology.

'It wouldn't be too far-fetched,' Paul wrote, 'to say he believes in those gods himself! In some of the cults and rituals he certainly believes. Would you credit it that I have seen him perform a ritual to make it rain and another that's supposed to make his apple trees bear fruit? He is quite crazy! But as kind to me as can be. Nothing is too much trouble for him and his staff to do for me.'

I asked her if she had written back.

'I wrote five letters in all. Not as long as his and, of course, without as much interesting stuff in them. Strange that, really, because I was the one who was living in London, in the centre of things, and he was in this small village out in the sticks, seeing the same people every day. But his letters were full of beauty and excitement, and mine – well, I never seemed to have anything to say. I used to try to find things to tell him. I remember in one letter I asked him how long his hair was. He'd said he was growing his hair, that Roche had asked him to grow it.'

'Asked him to grow his hair? But why?'

'Something about making himself look like Tezcatlipoca. Those people that made the Codex, they dressed up young men to look like the god and that meant having long hair.'

'Do you think Roche was …?'

'Interested in him sexually? No, I don't think so. You'll see why not if you read the rest.'

He wrote that he never went out alone. If ever he thought of taking a walk or driving into the village or into Exeter, Roche or one of the staff, Andrew or Peter, always said they would come, too. He was never alone, except at night. This was not a complaint, far from it, he was very happy, but it sometimes struck him as unusual, that was all.

Another strange thing was that there were very few books in the house, no fiction, no works of reference. A Spanish dictionary, yes, and a Nahuatl dictionary, and various art books of collections in museums that were of help in his cataloguing, but that was all. It was disappointing because he would have liked to read about the ceremonies that Roche spoke of. He would have liked to learn more about that culture.

Sometimes he thought that he was denied information that could easily have been obtained, but this he feared, was through ignorance. He suspected Roche – though it seemed disloyal to say so – of not fully knowing his subject, of not always being as accurate about some of these rituals and customs as a trained scholar would have been.

'Well, it will all be over in April,' he wrote, 'and then I will have plenty of chances to be lonely, no doubt! When my contract comes to an end at Easter I will be a free man.' He added, oddly, 'The truth is that I don't always feel quite free.'

The next letter to Rosie was sent in March. I read a few lines, set it down, and looked at her.

'What does he mean about the girls?'

'It's all there. I don't know any more than you do.' She took her eyes from my face. 'I wasn't in love with him and he wasn't in love with me. I suppose he thought it was all right to write like that to me – about things like that, I mean. I don't think I much liked it at the time. No woman would. But Paul was naive, wasn't he? He had terrific blind spots. Perhaps he felt he had to write to someone and there was no one else.' She said quickly, as if she wanted to get it said before thinking too much about it, 'Do you think he was a prisoner?'

'In Devon? In 1964?'

'There was no phone, you know. Roche didn't have a phone.'

The staff at Mandate House was joined by four girls, Paul wrote. Up till then there had been no women – it was months, nearly a year, since he had spoken to a woman apart from shop assistants. Roche introduced one of these girls to him 'in a special way!' She was to be his companion; he must be starved of female company. 'Look on her as your girlfriend,' Roche said. Writing about it to Rosie, Paul followed this piece of reported speech with three exclamation marks, but whether he took Roche up on this offer he omits to say.

After two more days a second girl showed an interest in him. One night she came to the door of the flat he had in a wing of the house and, when he let her in, went into his bedroom. That was all he said, that the girl he called Xilonan showed an interest in him, tapped on his door, and came into his bedroom. The other girls were not mentioned, and he went into no further details. There was nothing about his relations with one or all of these women, nothing more about 'female company' or special kinds of companionship.

Instead, he went on to write about an Easter celebration Roche was arranging. It was to coincide with the termination of Paul's contract and would centre on a ceremony, a rite that the Aztecs performed to ensure a good summer. No doubt, Roche said, he would fail to get the details right, but he would like to perform it as best he could with the help of Andrew, Peter, Nigel, and the girls – and of course, Paul. At worst it would rain and the whole thing have to be called off, at best it would be a very beautiful ceremony and perhaps something that could in future be performed as part of a festival. He even envisaged an annual event at Mandate House, attended either by the public or else by specially invited guests.

'He asked me what was I meaning to do after Easter. Go to Mexico, I said. Go and see my relatives in London first and then off to Mexico City. And what do you think he did? Next day he presented me with an air ticket! A bonus, he said, for what I'd done over and above the call of duty.

'We do the ritual on Easter Monday. They dress me up and the girls – he calls them my wives! – take formal leave of me, I climb up the steps of the temple and break a couple of ceramic flutes and no doubt Roche chants some mantra or rubric, and that it. Bob's your uncle! If all goes according to plan and it works, the sun will never stop shining! I'll send you a postcard from Aztec-land. With love, Paul.'

'He never did,' Rosie said, 'but people don't, do they, no matter what they say? And they disappear from one's life – but as utterly as that? From everyone's life?'

I asked her what she meant to do.

'What can I do? Worry for a while, I suppose, and then – I don't know.'

Paul Hazlitt was probably in Mexico still, or living in Australia, or a mile or two from us in London, married, with children. I told her that. And, no, it was not surprising that he had failed ever to get in touch. We all know how we feel about those we have lost contact with over a long period of time. We are afraid to break the silence, make the tentative approach, lest they are still sore, still hurt, and liable to lash back vindictively.

Whatever she said, I think she must have loved him, for her

face was full of woe. But in time, no doubt, she forgot him, as I did. I met a man and fell in love and married him. I married a man who knew as a professional what Paul's employer knew only as a dilettante. But Michael is no Declan Roche. For one thing, he has no money, or only what he earns teaching Latin American Studies at this university in the Midwest where we live, and the culture of the Aztecs is not his special subject. But he does, of course, know a good deal about them, as he does about all the ancient Mexica groups, and our house is full of books on Mesoamerica.

The passage I am going to quote in a minute came not from one of them but is Michael's own translation from the Spanish of a sixteenth-century friar. The friar must have interpreted one of the codices, perhaps even that which came into Roche's possession, and been a devout religious who saw the gods of Mexico as demons and their customs as barbaric. Michael's own view is rather different, dispassionate but inquisitive.

'The whole notion of men impersonating gods is fascinating,' he says. 'Of men *being* gods for a while. They made bloodless war, you see, and took captives, choosing the most beautiful, "without a single corporal blemish," to be the god. They taught him good manners and reverenced him.'

'But why?'

For answer he gave me this paper. He intends to use it in a book he is writing, just as he will use several other expositions of Aztec practices. Of course, I have told him about Paul and Roche and Mandate Benedict, but I have noticed an uncharacteristic lack of interest, due perhaps to Roche's amateur status. Michael is an academic and academics are always like that, distrustful and even contemptuous of the likes of Declan Roche. It was lucky, is his only comment, that the Mandate Codex came to no harm while in his hands.

All there is left for me to me to say is that I very much doubt if harm came to my second cousin once removed, Paul Hazlitt. I shall not be at all surprised if he turns up here one day at a symposium or to give a course of lectures on, say, Art in the Enlightenment or From Phidias to Giacometti. I would have paid no attention to the following translation but for the mention of the four women, one being named Xilonan, and the long hair ...

Twenty days before the feast, they removed the attire in which until then he had made penance, washing off the paint which he was used to wear. And they married him to four damsels, with whom he had conversation those twenty days that remained. They cut his hair in the way that was used by the captains and tied it in a little knot above his head. With a strange ribbon they tied to his hair two hangings with their decorations made from feathers and gold and rabbit skin, very strange, which they called aztxelli. *The four damsels whom they gave him as his women were also raised with great discernment. To that end they named them after four goddesses: one was called Xochiquetzal; another, Xilonan; the third, Atlatonan; and the fourth, Huixtocihuatl.*

Five days before reaching the feast, they honoured this youth like a god. The court followed him and, all richly attired, held solemn feasts and banquets. On the first day they fêted him in the ward known as Tecanman; the second in the ward where they kept the statue of Tezcatlipoca; the third on the little hill which they call Tepetzinco, which is in the lake; the fourth, on another island also in the lake called Tepepulco.

This fourth feast ended, they put him into a canoe in which the lord was accustomed to travel, covered with its own awning, and with

him his women who consoled him. And leaving Tepepulco, they navi-
gated towards a place called Tlapitzahuayan, which is near the road
to Itzapalapa, that goes towards Chalco, where is a little mound called
Acaquilpan or Cahualtepec. In this place his four women left him and
all the rest and returned to the city. He was accompanied only by the
pages who had attended him throughout the year.

They took him to a small cu or temple, poorly adorned, which was
at the side of the road outside the settlement, about a league distant
from the city. He himself ascended the steps of the temple, and on the
first level he broke into pieces one of the flutes which he had played in
the time of his prosperity, and on the second level he broke another,
and thus he went breaking them all, climbing the steps.

At the top of the cu the satraps were waiting. They cast him on the
stone, and, holding him by the arms and feet and head, thrown as he
was back on the altar, he who had the obsidian knife passed it through
his chest with one great slash. Into the opening thus made, the satrap
put in his hand, and wrenching out his heart, offered it to the Sun.

Trebuchet

This is the most important thing in life, she thought on waking, yet we never talk about it. When there is something frightening on the television, the radio, we switch off and we say, that's enough, it's too depressing. Or we used to say that. Now we switch off and say nothing, knowing what is in each other's minds.

He slept. He would sleep on for an hour or more. She had got into the habit of waking early when the children were babies and now she seldom slept on after five. Up here the sunrise came before that, it was so far north. The room was beginning to fill with a light that looked silvery because it was reflected off the sea. Every morning, for a long time now, her first thoughts had been of this kind, on the same theme. What will I do in the few minutes we shall be allowed? What shall I say to the children? If we are here on the island shall we be safe? If we had a boat we could escape northwards or westwards across the sea. Should I – and this was a question she baulked at, gagging on unuttered words – should I get something from the doctor? See if he would give me some very strong sleeping pills? And next time we go to the mainland should we buy a bottle, or two bottles, say, of very strong spirits? Looking down at Mark, she wondered how she could propose such a thing to him. And she imagined his look of stern disgust, under which fear hid.

In the nineteenth century it was sex people feared, in the early part of this one natural death. Those were what they shirked discussing. Now it was this. Whatever was the most important thing in life, that was what you shrank from. Mark could be dreaming of it now. She could tell he was dreaming, and not contentedly, his lips moving, his eyelids flickering, as if the Rapid Eye Movements of deep sleep were fierce enough to transmit a charge to the covering tissue. What she knew he must know. Teaching history was his job, writing his books a lucrative sideline. Better than she he must know that no nation had ever perfected a weapon and not used it. His dissertation for his Master's degree had been on the history of weapons. There were bits of it she still knew by heart:

Gravity is the force that powers the trebuchet, a great weight being attached to a pivoted beam near the heavy end. As the slender end is depressed the weight begins to rise, thus building a store of energy, and upon release the weight falls, sharply impelling upwards the long slender arm. A missile held in a sling at the end of this arm could be thrown great distances ...

Such devices and engines of destruction he had written of! Stone clubs, iron blades, crossbows and battering rams, ballistae, muzzle loaders and harquebuses, flintlocks, bayonets, mines, grenades, chlorine, napalm. No nation had ever perfected a weapon and not used it.

'Except germ warfare,' she had said. They could talk about *that*, still could. 'No country has ever used germs against another. I find that comforting.'

'Sorry to disillusion you then,' said Mark. 'The Germans have. They infected the horses of Romanian cavalry with glanders in 1914.'

In the next room a child called out. Cressy. Holidaying on the island, they woke early, they wanted to be out and about. She knew her train of thought would soon change, would thankfully veer away for another twenty-four hours to immediate domestic concerns, the children, Mark, the house, the garden and the day ahead. Cressy was out of bed, sitting on the floor, the contents of the toy chest sprawled around her. She had pulled back the curtains to let the sun in and drive Tim, head and all, under a cocoon of bedclothes.

The fine weather was in its second week now. You didn't expect it so it was all the more precious, a kind of bonus. The mainland was visible only on very clear days after rain and then as a dark blue line through which the artist has smudged his thumb. Today the horizon was lost in a pearly mist. The tiny islands, too small for habitation, lay scattered on the flat gleaming sea like fallen leaves on a sheet of marble. She looked down on to the garden, the fuchsia hedges, the roses in their second blooming, a dark purple clematis bearing so many hundreds of flowers that it hung over the wall like a curtain of tapestry, densely embroidered. Visitors marvelled at the lushness of it and had to be reminded that the west coast of Scotland was a warm place, that tropical gardens grew on Rum and palm trees at Gairloch. They forgot that the Gulf Stream came up here. Mark had written a thriller about the Gulf Stream, about a bathymetrist who found a way to divert its course and holding the countries of the Northern Hemisphere to ransom by his threats to do so. It was curious that the success of that book had enabled them to take a lease on this house and come up to stay here every July and August.

Tim surfaced from under the blankets and she took both children downstairs with her. At once the day impinged. There was the cat to be let in and the dog to be let out. Breakfast to get. Baking today and the bread to be made, kneaded, set to rise. She opened the windows, remembering the funny thing Tim had said about the air the first time they came, though they had known what he meant, that it was like spring water.

'Can I be the one to go and wake Daddy?'

Cressy had got in first. They vied with each other for this doubtful privilege, longed for perhaps because their requests were always refused unless there were some specific reason for getting Mark up before eight.

'No one is going to wake Daddy. He needs his sleep. He was working till late last night.'

Cressy accepted this without demur. Tim said he would like a fried egg.

'Could you fry my cornflakes?'

'No, I couldn't.'

'Why does it mean it's going to rain when cats wash behind their ears?'

'It doesn't,' said Tim.

'Yes, it does. It always rains when Chloe washes behind her ears.'

'She isn't washing behind her ears now. She's asleep.'

'There you are,' said Cressy. 'That proves it.'

It was a safe place, the island, without a cliff ledge or treacherous stream, surrounded by a sea that was limpidly shallow for a great way out. There was only one other house, a granite place with turrets where Willie Strachan their landlord lived. The island belonged to Willie, everything in this small kingdom belonged to him, the white pony in the meadow and the herd of goats, the motorboat he went in to the mainland every Monday. Everything except us, said Cressy, and Chloe and Jack. Willie would walk across from the big house soon, she thought, bringing the things he had promised to get for them, fresh fruit and yesterday's newspaper and batteries for the radio. She began to knead the bread dough, pummelling it with her knuckles and the heel of her hand, the sun falling on her in a cloak of hot brightness.

Mark walked in. He came up behind her, put his arms round her and kissed the corner of her mouth. She turned to him, smiling.

'Isn't it a wonderful day?'

He nodded. 'I haven't been in bed all this time. I've been down to the sea. Willie didn't come back last night. His boat's not there.'

'He doesn't always, not if the weather's bad.'

That made Cressy laugh. Tim said, 'Ooh, isn't it cold? Aren't you cold Cressy? It's raining, it's snowing.'

Cressy took this up with mock shivers and shouts about thunder and hailstones. They mimed sheltering from a storm, cowering and warding off imagined danger with their hands.

'Please don't do that!'

They were unaccustomed to their mother speaking sharply and their faces fell. They got up awkwardly.

'I'm sorry but I don't like to see you do that. Come along, it's time you were off outside.'

Mark closed the door behind them. 'That wasn't like you, Miriam. They were only playing.'

She said nothing. She covered the bowl of dough with a cloth and set it aside to rise. Back at the window, while Mark ate his breakfast, she looked out across the sea, searching for the boat that when it came would sear across that flat gleaming sheet like a diamond scoring glass. The sky was a blue bowl filled with light. The clarity of the air was such that it was as if everything, the still trees, the roses, even the pony and the prancing dog, were made of glass, spun, blown or stretched in filaments. She had to think then, spoiling the delight of it, that glass was of all substances the most easily broken.

Mark went off to work on his new book. It was about a scientist whose spaceship entered the magnetosphere where the northern lights are produced as, so to speak, an image on a gigantic screen, and how, for enormous financial gain, he had found a way to harness the auroral atoms. All the time they had been up here they had hoped to see the aurora, for as Mark said, how could he write about it unless he had seen it? And then, last night for the first time, they had. Miriam went out into the garden, down the lawn between the fuchsia hedges, to the spot where they had stood. 'A distinct greenish-white curtain-shaped light,' the encyclopaedia said, or a rayed band or corona, or crimson sometimes in the poleward sky. North-east of them it had certainly been but the light had been white and very brilliant and not much more than momentary, unfurling and flooding and bathing the heavens with an enormous radiance, dying quite soon to a red glow, to darkness. Empty the sky now was and empty the sea, the sun already fiercely hot. She went on across the meadow of flowering grasses, down to the beach where the children were.

He had written his 2,000 words for the day. They had their lunch outside, going without dessert because Willie hadn't brought the strawberries. A butterfly kept settling on Cressy's bright-red bathing costume, hung on a bush to dry, mistaking it for a flower. Miriam said it was a Red Admiral, though it wasn't, but velvet black with a white and scarlet pattern.

'I suppose he's decided to stay a day or two in Mallaig,' said Mark. 'That would happen just when the television's gone wrong.'

Groans from Cressy and Tim, cries of protest.

'We can phone the man,' said Tim.

'You forget that when we phone the man we have to go and fetch him or Willie does.'

'I do wish we had a boat,' said Cressy.

Miriam was more intent on accounting for Willie's absence. 'As a matter of fact I can see clouds coming up on the skyline.'

Mark could too. 'Behold, there ariseth out of the sea a little cloud no bigger than a man's hand.'

She looked at him queerly. 'Is that the Bible? Before the flood or something?'

'I don't think so, only rain coming to Elijah.'

And to us before the day is out, he thought later, as the hand expanded to an arm, to massive shoulders and whole bodies of cloud, at last to an amorphous coating, thick and black, hiding the sky. Inevitably up here that meant rain. If it confined the children indoors they would need television. He tried to phone the engineers on the mainland but the phone was dead. When Willie came back they could use the phone at the house.

But would he come now? By teatime the light was dim. A false dusk had come. Miriam got the children to bed and Mark walked outside. In spite of the thick crust of cloud the sea was glassily calm still, yet with a swell it seemed to rock it from beneath like water carried in an overfull dish. The weather was exactly that which preceded a summer storm except in one respect. Usually in these conditions the blossoming shrubs and plants looked brighter in colour, more intensely activated in light, so that they glowed with a pale luminosity. This evening, though, iridescence was lacking and the lilacs and reds and rich pinks leeched of colour and silky sheen, only the sea gleaming like the scaly skin of some great reptile.

Sunset would come late. He went back outside at ten but he couldn't see a pinpoint of it, no thin streak or split in the piled cumulus. On the mainland shore were a few twinkling lights. Fallen stars, Cressy had once called them, gazing from her bedroom window. Mark, who had been feeling uneasy, was tremendously buoyed up by the sight of these fallen stars.

Going in, he said to Miriam, 'Do you know where the radio is? There might be something on it about this freak weather.'

He felt that she clutched at that, relieved that this was why he wanted the radio. 'It's in the living room, in the cupboard.'

If I could get some news, he thought, I wouldn't mind finding out what's happening in Germany. Of course it will all have calmed down by now, these things always do. He found the radio and carried it out to the kitchen, expecting to find Miriam still there but she had gone. It was odd how the memory came to him, flashing up suddenly, triggered by he didn't know what, of himself as a boy and the crisis over Cuban missiles at its height, and every time his father switching on for the news his mother going out of the room on some excuse. Ostriches, ostriches all. Later on, for a while, he'd gone on marches, even sat down outside the gates of some base whose name he'd forgotten – but what good did it do? Only if the great mass of the people, the majority would rise and cry with one voice, No! Only then would something be done.

But you were one of them, an inner voice uttered, and the whole is the sum of its parts. He told it to shut up and switched on the radio. There was crackling and a hissing sound, the interference that sounds like paper tearing, an ensuing silence and out of it, dear and slow, a woman's voice:

'Oh God, help us all …!'

That was all he was to hear. The pounding rushing noise which followed sounded as if the waves of the sea were being recorded. He went to find Miriam.

'I got a bit of a radio play and then the battery gave out.'

She nodded. 'Still, that's good, isn't it?' It was a curious thing to say, meaningless unless you understood ostrich psychology.

'Would you like a nightcap? There's some rather good cognac. I had Willie get us a bottle.'

She looked at him quickly, then away. 'I don't think so, Mark. I'll have a hot drink.'

Neither of them could get to sleep. It had grown cold. Mark thought of Tim and Cressy miming winter weather in the hot sun at breakfast time, an accurate prevision if ever there was one, and he got up at half-past midnight, went into their room and put extra blankets on them. The night was pitch black and on the distant coast the twinkling lights had gone out, the fallen stars had been extinguished – but there hardly would be lights at this hour. It was not at all warm in the bedroom yet a condensation that was more than a mist, that was running water drops, had formed on the window panes.

We are safe enough here, he said to himself, not specifying even in his thoughts. This will be a sanctuary, a kind of deep shelter. The aurora's white corona flowered again in his mind's eye, the voice emerging from torn paper, crying for God's help fell again on his ear, but there could be no talking of those things to Miriam. While they remained unuttered they would still hover uneasily in their thin disguises, as a phenomenon of the magnetosphere, as an actress reading a part.

'Are you awake?'

Miriam sat up. 'Has it got very cold or is it my imagination?'

'It's pretty cold.'

'I suppose it's been raining. That would make it cold.'

'I don't think it's been raining.' He hesitated. 'Shall we take a sleeping pill? There's no point in lying awake.'

'We haven't got any sleeping pills.'

'Well, yes, we have as a matter of fact. I got some from the doctor a while back.'

He had a look of embarrassment. She turned away her face. Everything must be all right because their lights were working. Then she remembered that their electricity supply came off Willie's generator. Mark gave her a capsule and she swallowed it. The way sleep came was blissful, sensuous, like warm sweet milk pouring into an empty cup. She had no dreams. Afterwards, next day, she was to think that it was as if death had come already, or rather, that they were having a rehearsal for death so that they would know what it was like.

The children had to wake them up, they slept so late. The morning was dark, the sky leaden. Mark said he didn't suppose Willie would come today either and was going on to say more, about the weather and the sea, but Miriam's look of grim scorn, of contempt almost, silenced him. Tim and Cressy put on coats and scarves and boots and went outside. Mark felt that perhaps he should stop them, he should keep them in, but he could find no words to speak that weren't terrifying, wouldn't admit his fear.

He sat at the breakfast table, eating nothing. Somehow he knew Miriam had eaten nothing either, though there were crumbs on the children's plates. They had the kitchen light on. He had said nothing since that remark about Willie and she had said nothing to him and he felt he might never speak to her again, for he couldn't say what he wanted to, he was too afraid, and everything else seemed not worth saying. After a while she got up and put her coat on and holding the dog by his collar, went out into the garden. Mark went after her because he didn't want to be alone.

A preternaturally high tide had washed the shores of the island during the night, leaving behind it shoals of dead fish and corpses of birds. With serious faces and in silence Tim and Cressy contemplated these hecatombs sacrificed to an unknown god. They were too cold to linger, their teeth chattering. They slipped and slithered as they climbed back up the slope, as the turf was coated with a white rime.

'It must have snowed,' said Tim but he didn't think it had, for the stone-paved path was clear and dry as a bone.

'Did snow make the fishes dead?'

'Why do you always ask me? I don't know everything.'

The pony lay on its side in the frosty field. Tim couldn't see the goats anywhere and somehow he didn't want to. That could wait for later. He had a strange new feeling, the first of its kind he had ever had, that he must stop Cressy going nearer to the pony, because of his seniority he must *protect* her. This was a word his parents used and now he understood it. His age of reason had started, these were its doomed beginnings.

'Come on. Mummy said not to be long.'

They came upon their mother and father in the garden. Whatever it was that had blasted the birds and the fish had blown its cold breath on the roses. They hung down their brown and shrivelled heads. The fuchsia blossoms were encased in capsules of ice like glass beads. The Red Admiral still clung to a petal, frozen there, glued by a white lacy adhesive of ice.

Miriam was saying over and over that frost was impossible unless the sky was clear. Mark didn't answer her or attempt to argue about it. What did it matter, that rule of meteorology, when here the frost was? A cold windless silence prevailed. The mainland shore was no longer visible, for the sky, lowering, curdled and dark like smoke, seemed to have fallen over the horizon, making a blurred fusion of water, land and fog. Miriam, in a thin high voice, began speaking words he recognised as coming from his thesis. He heard her with horror, kneeling down on the icy ground as she spoke, putting an arm round each child, drawing them to him.

'As the slender end is depressed the weight begins to rise, thus building a store of energy, and upon release the weight falls, sharply impelling upwards the long slender arm. A missile held in a sling at the end of this arm could be thrown great distances …'

'Let's go in,' he said, though he knew that indoors it was to be no warmer and soon scarcely lighter.

In the kitchen the cat sat washing behind her ears and the dog whined softly. No sooner had Mark closed the door than the fallen heavens opened and the hail began, a crashing of ice stones that pounded upon the house, a cataract of ice plates and ice nuggets that descended on the frost-bitten garden, masking it in glittering broken glass. It was Tim who said that, peering out until it got too dark to see.

'It's like broken glass, the world is made of broken glass.'

'Rain of glass,' said Cressy, stroking the cat. 'And that proves it. It does mean it's going to rain.' She hugged herself. 'Mummy, I'm cold.'

And Mark, who had been staring out at his deep shelter, his shelter in the deep, came away from the window and his tongue freed at last, touched Miriam's white face, spoke into her ear:

'This is it. They have done it.'